Cora Linn V. S. Richmond, Ouina

Ouina's Canoe and Christmas Offering

filled with flowers for the darlings of earth

Cora Linn V. S. Richmond, Ouina

Ouina's Canoe and Christmas Offering
filled with flowers for the darlings of earth

ISBN/EAN: 9783337380540

Printed in Europe, USA, Canada, Australia, Japan

Cover: Foto ©Andreas Hilbeck / pixelio.de

More available books at **www.hansebooks.com**

OUINA'S CANOE

AND

CHRISTMAS OFFERING.

Filled with Flowers for the Darlings
of Earth

Given through her Medium.
"WATER LILY."
(MRS. CORA L. V. RICHMOND.)

OTTUMWA, IOWA.
D. M. & N. P. FOX. PUBLISHERS.
1882.

DEDICATION.

TO THE LITTLE PEOPLE,

THE DARLINGS OF EARTH, FOR WHOM THESE STORIES AND

POEMS WERE GATHERED FROM MY GARDEN,

I DEDICATE THIS LITTLE BOOK.

OUINA.

CONTENTS.

PREFACE.

—>⟩≡⟨←—

This canoe, or little book, laden with flowers for the little ones, is the first *book* I have ever sent out. Many stories and poems have I written and spoken; more than fifty volumes would contain, and if my little canoe pleases you dear children, another will follow.

These are but wayside flowers; all my own garlands of a year, strung together without any special reason only to tell of the beautiful in everything, and lead the mind from *forms* and *words* of beauty, to the soul of the beautiful, which is divine.

Trusting my little boat to the streams and harbors of your loving thoughts, I send it forth as my " Christmas Gift," and my wish for a " Happy New Year " to you all.

OUINA.

OUINA'S CANOE

AND

CHRISTMAS STORIES.

DEDICATORY.

HAVE you seen the bright new moon.
Resting at twilight in the sky—
Did it not seem a white canoe
Floating out from the world on high?
The silver moon is my canoe
In which I bring bright flowers to you.

Have you seen it like a bended bow
Held by an unseen hand in heaven.
While silver arrows speed below
Swiftly. to light your way at even?
The bended bow is of Truth above.
The arrows are the rays of Love.

Have you seen the stars come forth
Like buttercups or daisies bright.
And twinkle softly toward the earth,
Kindling the darkness with their light?
The stars are like the angels' eyes
That shine on you from Paradise.

Have you watched for the flowers of spring
 And seen the leaves and buds unfold—
And heard the wild birds twittering—
 And spied the cowslips full of gold?
  Your budding thoughts are, like the spring,
  And are like flowers the angels bring.

Have you seen the young bird try to fly,
 And overhead and all around
The parent birds forever nigh-
 To teach, to aid if on the ground?
  So do your parents strive to guide—
  So are your angels by your side.

Have you seen the rain-drops patter down,
 And send you home and spoil your play,
And did you pause and with a frown
 Wish all the rain would go away?
  Raindrops are blessings to the flowers-
  And tears often cleanse eyes like yours.

Have you ever watched the fleecy clouds
 Like troops of shining angels come,
And think of little sister there
 Or darling brother in that home?
  And when you think of them as dead
  Theyr'e close beside you here instead.

Have you ever felt like praying then
 A little prayer for those you love—
For those who have no love? And when
 You ask God's blessing from above,
  Your prayer is like a star from heaven,
  Or white flower by an angel given.

And did you ever think a thought
  Or do a loving deed at play,
That made you softly sing and shout
  And feel so happy all the day?
      Your little angel friends come near
      When you are kind and loving here.

So my canoe and all my flowers
  Must be the white thoughts that I bring,
Must be those loving messages,
  Must be these songs that I shall sing,
      And if I have sweet thoughts from you
      I'll take them home in my canoe.

My home is in the spirit state,
  I live with angels in their home,
And what we have we must create;
  So this is why to earth I come.
      We build our homes with thoughts above,
      We plant our bowers with seeds of love--

Not in the clouds, or stars, or moon,
  But in your minds and in your hearts
I come. And you shall know me soon
  By what my love to you imparts.
      So let my meaning glimmer through
      Pure thoughts must be my white canoe.

THE STORY OF OUINA'S EARTH LIFE.

MORE than three hundred " harvest moons,* ago my people lived where the head waters of the Shenandoah river rise, and their hunting grounds were the valley through which that river runs. My sire was the Chief of the Shenandoah nation and they took their name, as did the river, from him. They were a peaceful people, their only foes being the Kanawah's, who lived to the westward and who sometimes made war for plunder or revenge on my father's people ; but it had been many years since there had been war among them, and our people were prosperous and happy; The Great Spirit, "Gitchu Manitou," had given them the hunting grounds and the river ; these yielded game and fish for food, the bear and deer skins and those of all the beasts they killed for food, served for the wigwams, while from the bark of the birch tree and from strong skins and the pitch of the pine tree, they made their canoes for the councils.

*A harvest moon is a year.

Twice each harvest moon they journeyed to the sea shore to gather shells for "wampum" and sea fish for food, then back again to the shelter of the hills they would go until the time came for another journey to the sea. Once when our people were by the sea there came up a great storm, a mighty Manitou of terror swept over the waters, they saw a great white bird with white wings come toward the land, then they saw it go down into the dark waters never to rise again ; they believed it was the Spirit of the Storm. But when the clouds were gone and the morning sun shone again my sire saw a woman floating along on the water, and the waves brought her to the shore. She could not speak with fear and exhaustion, but the women placed her on a bed of soft skins and warmed her and gave her food, and the medicine man brought healing herbs, and she was soon able to speak, but her words were strange. She was very beautiful and my sire made her his wife, loving her tenderly, and bringing her every offering from the ocean, every gift of love. The women loved her and believed as my sire did, that she was sent by "Manitou," the Great Spirit, to be his wife; they almost worshiped her, and the fame of her beauty and goodness spread far and wide.

But she pined and grew paler every day, although she never murmured, my sire told me

she would go to a stream near the wigwam each
morning and evening and chant a strange, sweet
hymn. She learned to know the language of
our people, and told them of a land far over
the sea where her people dwelt, and that the
ship on which she came, had white sails, and
that it was built like a huge canoe, that her
father was chief (commander) of the ship, and
that all on board perished in the storm; her sire
strapped her to a mast as the ship sank to rise
no more, and she floated to the shore. She
told them of God, the Manitou her people
worshiped, and showed them a cross she wore
on her bosom, as the symbol of the love of Jesus for the world.

My sire wondered and worshiped afar off
these strange, new thoughts, but he did not
understand them, and when after one harvest
moon my mother died, I was left to comfort
him. My mother's name was Cleona, (the rose
with the bleeding heart,) for she died of hem-
orrhage of the lungs, and my people believed
the blood came from the heart.

As my eyes opened to earth life my mother
breathed her last on earth. My childhood
was among the scenes of Nature, in my father's
wigwam I had a warm bed of skins and dried
moss and leaves to rest upon; I had a seat
made of a pine log covered with skins, I had
bright berries and leaves and feathers and
stones and shells for my "wampum."

I could not eat the flesh of bird or fish or meat of any kind; whatever had to be slain I could not eat, so I gathered wild fruit and nuts and corn (which was planted around the wigwams) and lived on these.

The birds would come at my call, for I could imitate their songs, and they would float around me knowing I would do them no harm. The wild deer would feed from my hand, and even the bears would not touch me to do me harm, but would go away. I walked a long way in the forest alone without fear, and my people said a Manitou went with me.

At twilight I would go to the stream where my mother used to go, and there I would hear her voice singing the anthem she used to sing on earth; my people would hear the voice also and never came near lest they should harm me and drive the spirit of my mother away. The following is the hymn my mother sang, and that her spirit taught me the meaning of :

O, sacred mother, hear thou thy daughter's prayer.
O, Jesus hear me, for thou art every-where.
Here in the forest, O God, my King,
Thy humble worshiper homage will bring.

O Heavenly Friend, bend near, I am exiled, alone,
Stoop thou kindly to hear from thy bright throne.
Let me not murmur, nor doubt thy love.
O take me home to thee, to thy world above.

Each evening I would hear this song and I
soon learned it, but it was in another language, and my sire did not know its meaning.
I would like to tell you of all my happy childhood ; how the little squirrels were my friends,
and would chatter and crack their nuts above
my head in the trees, and how the ground
mole and the owls would under stand what
I said to them.   I want you to know all this,
for if you are kind to everything, nothing will
harm you.

This is what the birds and leaves used to
sing :

SWEET, sweet, sing to us sweet,
　　Here comes the Red Chief's daughter.
　She will not harm us, her tender feet
　　Glide over flowers; O the sweet water
Sings like her voice so sweet, so sweet,
　　　Te wheet, te wheet.
　　　Fro rol, to rol, sweet.

Rustle, shiver and clap your hands.
　All of you leaves together,
For she will wreath you in crimson bands,
　In the golden autumn weather:
Never a flower she plucks from its stem,
　Never a leaf for her garment's hem,
　　Rustle and fall
　　At her feet, one and all.

Chatter, chatter, how do you do ?
　Switch your tails merrily,

For see she comes. let her pass through,
   For she sings and talks so cheerily:
Squirrel, dormouse and mole.
Hasten come out of each hole:
      Chatter, to hoot. chatter.
      O. what a merry clatter."

One twilight as I thus held communion with the spirit of my mother. there came a strange message from the hunting grounds of the spirit world. She told me in that message that my father's people would be scattered like the leaves of the forest in autumn when swept by the wind: that the mighty Kanawah had rallied all his forces from the west-land (West Virginia and the Ohio,) and they would come down upon us with great warfare, like mighty war-birds, slaying and scattering the braves and warriors of Shenandoah. She told me that the hunters and warriors from the spirit land saw mighty sea-canoes, with white wings like huge sea-birds come across the great ocean bearing pale faced warriors like her people, and these would drive all the Red men away, taking their hunting grounds and their streams. Then my mother sang the hymn I told you of before, and blessing me, she went away to her home in the spirit.

The women in the door of their wigwams heard her voice. I saw her form depart, and saw my own form in the stream; it was like hers only more slender.

The next morning my sire summoned me to the place beside him in the council; I forebore to speak, I had not slept all night fearing the effect of the message upon him.

"Why is my daughter sad, why does the Lily of the forest droop and grow pale? The Manitou spoke with her by the stream, and the sweet voice was heard in all the glen of the song to the Great Spirit, speak daughter, and naught shall harm you."

"O, my sire, I speak to you truly, but I have been silent lest my message should grieve you or turn your heart from your child, but this I saw and heard: My mother came beside the stream as is her wont at twilight; I saw her form, I heard her voice more plainly than ever before; she said: "Tell your sire the message from the hunting grounds of the Manitou is of danger; tell him Kanawah comes with many mighty warriors from the west-land to slay his people; tell him they will be scattered like the leaves of the forest, that the great Shenandoah and his people will perish; tell him the white sails come from the far-sea country, from the land of my own earth people; tell him there is sorrow to his councils, but he is brave and Manitou will reward him." Sire this was all I heard; she sang to me the music of praise; she blessed me and then she went away."

In the council were the braves, warriors

and chiefs; in the wigwams the women were
preparing for a feast: my sire spoke no word;
he waved his hand to the council; he rose and
left the people, I followed him but he did
not speak to me, he spoke no word, he ate no
food; the feast was not prepared; the braves
remained a little way off and the chiefs held
counsel together. For three days and nights
my sire was silent. For three days and nights
he spoke not to his daughter. The women
shunned me, the chiefs looked angry at me,
the braves were afar off, but one watched and
guarded my footsteps; he was the fleetest, he
was the bravest hunter, he was a valiant war-
rior ; alas, I did not know what was coming; I
wandered in the forest by day and sought my
lonely home at night, then the women would
pity me and say: "Her sire has turned from
her, what will the Forest Lily do?"

Seven days and nights had passed and my sire
had neither slept nor partaken food; then he
called a council; then he bade the fires be lighted; then he summoned all the chiefs, braves
and warriors together. The women stood
afar off or in their tents and pitied me, for my
sire did not summon me to the council nor
did he speak to his child. My sire broke silence
and said :

"Sachems and warriors; as the fawn to the
hart, as the young eaglet to the parent bird,
as the moon to the night, as the arrow to the

bow of the hunter, so was the child, the daughter of the chief, to her sire. The light of his
eyes, the sunshine of his heart, the only joy of
his life; she could not hunt, she could not
go to war, she could not be a chief in our
councils, but she was more, for Manitou gave
her the form of a woman but the soul of a God,
and she saw with the eyes of the spirit and heard
the counsels of Manitou; our councils have been
guided by wisdom, our people have prospered,
our hunters have brought plenty of game
and we have had corn and also food from the
sea; but now, alas! she brings a message of woe;
Manitou the good has deserted us, she has
no word of cheer for her sire, no praise for
the warriors; she has been visit by a Manitou
of evil. I saw in the eye of a white eagle the
sign; I waited seven suns for the sign; it means
death.

Warriors, the heart of your chief is broken,
but he will not weep like a woman; his Lily, his
fawn, must be taken from him for his people
and their welfare, else this spirit of darkness,
this Manitou who comes to harm you, will
drink the life blood of my people."

Thus spoke my sire and sat down. One
arose in council when my sire had finished;
young and slender, his form swayed like the
young forest tree, his words were full of fire:

"Why should the Lily perish? Why slay
one so young and tender? The very flowers

love her, the birds answer her calling, the
squirrels come to meet her; even the serpent
fears her and hides his sting and venom; she
has been kind and lovely, has done no wrong
to any. O, chiefs, why should we slay her?
Take back the cruel edict!" And the young
braves responded: " Let not the Lily perish;
slay not your only daughter "

But the chiefs and sachems gathered around
my sire and answered: "The mighty chief
hath spoken." And my sire said: "I have
spoken!"

Then twenty young braves were chosen,
the surest in the hunt; they were bade to pre-
pare their arrows in the poison of the man-
drake ; and the squaws (weeping and wailing)
were made to bring the fagots and pile them
near the hemlock, (they wept and moaned for
me then, and called me "murdered princess.")

The women took my clothing and heaped
it on the faggots, my robes and furs and all
things, they left but one poor blanket, a girdle
around my body, they were commanded and
must obey. They wound my long hair around
the hemlock tree; they touched the faggots,
and the twenty were commanded to fire their
arrows; nineteen arrows pierced my form, one
brave, (he who had spoken in the council
pleading for my life,) fired into the air and
sprang into the flames perishing with me. I

suffered no pain, my mother's spirit received
me.

Thus ended the earthly life, and together the
young brave and I passed to the hunting
grounds of the spirit. The shock of death was
not painful for my mother's presence had taken
away outward consciousness before the arrows pierced my body or the fiery tongues had
consumed. Gently, lovingly my mother drew
me to her, but I could not rest in her love
alone, I still had a duty to perform..

When the deed was finally accomplished
and the death fires were kindled, when the fast-
ings and feastings were ended, my sire was
stricken with fear, and ere many suns had rolled
away the mighty Kanawah and his hosts came
pouring in upon them. Like icicles were
their arrows, like red clouds at sunset were
their plumes, on and on they came, hiding in
the thickets, picking off one by one the bravest
of the warriors of Shenandoah; as leaves scattered by the wind, as the forest trees shattered
in the blast, such were my kinsmen, such were
the people of my sire; then others fell sick
and game was scarce, and in summer time the
streams in the mountains were dry. Weary
and worn and full of remorse, my sire turned
his footsteps with a small band of followers to
ward the place where he had sacrificed his child
and when the autumn sun shone red and golden on the hemlock tree, when the last ray

departed, he laid his head upon a stone and
died, his spirit passing to the land of the spirit.
"He died of a broken heart—of great grief,
remorse and loneliness."

The first to receive him was I, his daughter;
he covered his face with his hands to shut out
the vision of his murdered child, but I smiled
upon him and more and more won him from
his desolation, covering him with the flowers
of forgivness, with the soft mantle of charity,
until he sank away into peaceful rest, to rise
at last into usefulness and joy. For many
moons of earth (although we do not count
time by moons in spirit) I ministered to him
and he was healed of the sickness of sorrow,
for many moons I shared the labor of the
young brave who gave up his life rather than
slay the "Lily of the forest," and together we
passed on from the hunting grounds of my sire
to the house of my mother, she named me then
Ouina (lost and found one) and there, doing
good to others, and to those on earth and in
states beneath that required my care, I commenced the garden of the spirit, the home I
have often described to you. Many harvest
moons have come and gone, but if you visit the
head waters of the Shenadoah, you will see a
mound shaped like a cone on which is a thick
growth of forest trees; this mound is my mon-
ument, for whenever my people passed to and
from the sea shore, they cast a stone where I

was slain in memory of "the wounded Princess
of the Shenadoah," and when you cross the
river of death I will stand with my white canoe
to bear you to the home of Ounia.

A REQUIEM TO OUINA.

[Sung over her grave.]

THE FLOWERS SING.

SLEEP maiden sleep, the lily blooms o'er thy bed,
The violet's dewdrops weep, serving for tears instead:
The Rose would cast its bloom upon thy ashes here,
And light thy early tomb with incense pure and clear:
Sleep, maiden sleep.

THE WATERS SING.

Rest maiden rest, we would sing a lullaby
Soft as the mother's note, soft as the sound of the sea,
We would murmur o'er thy bed such songs of dear delight,
Each drop would crown thy head with a jewel of clear
light:
Rest maiden rest.

THE BIRDS SING.

Sweet, O folded sweet, silent thy voice of song,
No more its sounds we meet by the breezes born along:
Afar in the solitude the nightingale would moan,
We sing and chant thy praise, rest thou, O, loved one;
Sweet, rest thou sweet.

THE PINE TREE SINGS.

Moan, O pines make moan, soft sing your requiem here,

The solemn monotone of this most saddened year.
But softly waft the sound to the sky and air above.
There is the soul enwound, there must her spirit move:
　　Sing, pine trees, sing.

THE OCEAN SINGS.

Praise, waters move and praise, the wonders of the deep.
Your voice in anthems raise,not where the form doth sleep.
But where in waves of sound ye reach her charmed soul,
O let your songs abound, O let your anthems roll:
　　Sing, ocean roll and sing.

ALL NATURE SINGS.

Rejoice, sing and rejoice in a song of love and death.
For this is heaven's voice beyond all mortal breath:
Sing flowers, birds and trees, sing nature, sing ye stars,
Be vocal Pleiades! sing, fiery breath of Mars!
　　Rejoice for death, rejoice.

THE SOUL SINGS.

Immortal praise and love to the giver of all good.
Ruler in realms above, soul of the solitude:
A promise of life I bring, through death to life above.
The soul would ever sing in peans of purest love:
　　Sing, soul, Oh, spirit sing.

A FAIRY STORY.

A SILVERY moonbeam belated, gleamed upon a stream and floated into a drop of dew; resting there until all its sister moonbeams had passed on through the sky, then from the east there came a fiery dragon, his eyes were orbs of fire, his tail was a flame of fire. The fairy trembled, for she could not find her way again back to the moonbeams. Presently the young Dawn came and the Morning Star, still the dragon was in the east and the Fairy of the moonbeam waited to see the life of the Dawn and the Morning Star swallowed up by the dragon; presently the sun came and one faint Sun-beam fell where the moonbeam fairy faint with fear waited.

"What art thou here, fairy of the moonbeam?" he said. "I was belated and now I cannot find my home," said she.

"Why didst thou loiter, the moonbeam is for night and now the day will blast thy loveli-

ness and thy hour for labor is o'er," said he.
But I dread more the fiery dragon by your
eastern sky. Foolish Fairy; yonder fiery
dragon is but a comet flying through space;
the dawn was not afraid nor was the Morning
Star; I will light thee to thy home, but never
tarry again for thy sweetness is for the night."
So the Sunbeam bore her to her home and
never again did the Fairy of the moonbeam
wander, but her image is in the dew.

THE ISLAND OF LIGHT.

IN MY beautiful home is the "Island of Light"
    Surrounded by waters so blue.
And up the bright strand the waves with delight
    Pulsate into pearl-drops so true.

There are pure rays that fall from the Sun of all Truth,
    And spirits are bathed in those beams;
There are vallies of verdure and fountains of youth.
    And the forms that you see in love's dreams;

There are musical waters that evermore flow
    To refresh every flower in its bloom;
There are fruits, red and golden, that evermore grow,
    And no death, and no darkness, nor gloom;

There are fairy-like forms, and sweet faces and eyes,
    All tender with love-light and bliss,

And gleamings of splendor in love's paradise,
   Fulfillment of hope's honeyed kiss:

There are gondolas passing for aye to and fro,
   Bearing souls to the Island of Light:
And all whom you love—most whom you know—
   Are seeking that region so bright.

There are grottoes of prayer and white temples of thought,
   Dedicated to the Soul of all Truth:
There are forms of white beauty love hath outwrought,
   And images fashioned of youth.

The "Island of Light" is the home in the soul:
   Its palaces fashioned of deeds,
Its waters are thoughts that eternally roll:
   Its flowers, love has planted the seeds.

Around it the waves of eternity flow,
   Its shining sands are spirit states,
And the vallies of verdure are beauties that grow
   In the spirit by time's shadowed gates.

Its mountains are praises, aspirations, and works
   For the welfare of others below:
Its grottoes and temples are life's purest toil,
   Its forms are the loved whom you know.

Little children, the gondolas are your white thoughts,
   Passing into and out of the soul,
And freighted with beauty, and blessing are fraught
   To win you to that blessed goal.

O, Island of Light! O, waters of love!
   We seek thee forever on earth,
And forever our life-bark toward you must move.
   We are there in the spirit's new birth.

A STORY OF OUINA'S HOME.

OUINA.—"Who am I ?"

CHILDREN.—"Ouina, a Spirit"

O.—"Where do I live?"

C.—"In heaven.'

O.—"What did I promise to-day?"

C.—"A story of your world."

O.—'Yes, I promised you a story of my world, and my world is the spirit world; can you see it?"

C.—"No."

O.—"Why?"

C.—"Because it is so far away."

O.—"No, not that, but because it is so fine; you cannot see the air, yet it moves the trees, so my home is made of such etherial substance you cannot see it with mortal eyes. Have any mortals ever seen heaven? Yes, the Bible tells of 'visions' of heaven seen by prophets and seers, and there are those in the world to-day, who see spirit scenes and the spirits who dwell there; so my world *is* far away, but it is also near, and is not a star, but is formed of such substance as thoughts. I made my world, how do you suppose I made it?

C.—"By doing good."

O.—"Yes, by doing good to others; so you all make your heavenly homes. Now, I will tell you a true story about

LITTLE HARRY.

He lived in your world, and was well, and bright and happy, but he took a cold, was very ill and died (you may all have known of some little playmate or brother or sister who has died, so if I tell you about little Harry, who passed into our spirit world, you will know what it means.)

Well, Harry died, that is, his body did, but his spirit was alive and stood just outside of his body; and there too, were many spirits, his Grandmamma and others, who came to greet him, but Harry could see his body lying there and his mother and father and friends weeping over the casket, but they could not see him, nor could they see the bright spirits that were there to receive him. Harry tried to speak to his mamma, but she was too sad to hear him, for grief makes the ears deaf to angel voices. Well, his Gradmamma brought him to my world; it is a beautiful world, floating in space and bright with a light of its own—the light of the spirit. But Harry at first felt lonely and wanted to see his mamma, but he saw many happy children and many beautiful flowers, at first he thought *he* had no flowers there, (I mean none he could call his own,) but on one of the lovely islands a bright bed of flowers greeted Harry and he thought he knew them; now, when I say he thought he knew them, I mean they were his—his thoughts and deeds before he came to the spirit world. One flower, brighter than the rest, he chose for his mamma and thought he would take it to her; why he took that flower I will tell you; it was one he had planted in the garden of his spirit on a special day. When he was on the earth, one day he wanted to play, and his mamma had something she wanted him to do; how very much he wished to play with his mates and go with them on that special sport. His mamma had great need of him, and after quite a struggle in his own mind, he gave up his play, and his love for his mamma triumphed over his selfish desire. That flower which he now chose for his mamma, was planted then; he took it to her, but she was weeping and planting earthly flowers upon his grave. Harry laid the flower he had brought, upon her bosom, she began to feel better, as though a heavy load had been taken from her heart, and she thought of that *very day* when Harry was *so* good and helped her when he wanted to play, she almost felt as though he was there; and so he was, could she but have seen him. When Harry

came to his spirit home for spirits pass to and
fro at will, if you wish a drink of water or to
go and play, your spirit moves your body to
do it; spirit bodies are lighter and finer and
move readily by the power of the will or wish,
he found a dozen flowers blooming in the place
of the one he had taken.   I will tell you more
of what Harry did in my world and of the islands he visited.   We have here the Island of
Light, the Island of Pearl, the Islands of Lilies and Roses and Violets, and all are filled
with little people like you.

They are taught, but not in books.   The
flowers, birds and lovely forms are made from
their thoughts and good deeds.

CHAPTER II.

HARRY'S VISIT TO THE "ISLAND OF LIGHT" THROUGH THE "RAINBOW ARCH."

FTER Harry had become accustomed to his new home and to his flower garden, other lessons and pleasures were given him—for the work and play are the same in spirit life, every deed being a pleasure because it is good or useful for others. As a lesson and pleasure, therefore, an excursion was planned to the "Island of Light." From the different islands and from all parts of the spiritual garden, came companions who were to accompany Harry. May, Lily, Violet, Rose, Pearl, Ruby, Jasper (for some spirits have the names of gems,) and many more. The guardian of the day was a messenger from the Island of Light, who had come to take the little ones there. They went in small boats—white, to symbolize *pure thoughts*, or blue, to express *wisdom*—and passed directly through the Rainbow Arch, you see it pictured there (pointing to a picture in the room.) "The Rainbow Arch," said the guardian, "is formed

of sympathy, the tears you shed for another's
sorrow.   When you see a rainbow in the sky,
it is because upon the dark back-ground of
clouds, the rays of the sun, shining through
the rain, are reflected; so upon the dark clouds
of sorrow the light of love and sympathy
shines, and through tears the rainbow of hope
is seen.   This archway is sympathy."

As Harry and the others were borne along
the clear water (symbol of truth) reflected
every image, and above his head Harry saw
one span of the archway, on which his name
"Harry," was written.   It was *his* span of the
archway and was formed of his sympathy for
one of his mates in earth life when that mate
was in sorrow.   So you little ones will find
your names on some rainbow arch in spirit
life, for every tear you shed in sympathy for
others, builds that arch for you.

On and on they went, the way growing
more bright and dazzling, but it was not the
light of the sun, it was the light of truth; the
light of those wise ones who dwell on the Island of Light.   Harry and the other children
were, at first, almost overcome by such brightness.   They saw shining temples of light and
palaces all filled with splendor.   Harry walked
a little way alone and came to a small pavilion, very white and bright and this was his
own, he saw his name written there and he
saw how he had built it—by *love of truth*, for

Harry's mother remembered (she all the while weeping for him on earth) that he had never told her anything but the truth, so he found his own dear little temple in this Island of Light (or Truth.) Then all the children came to a large bright place, where there were many spirits. Harry saw some he whom he knew, they seemed to be making chains or wires of light; they wondered what these were for. The guardian told them to watch and think and they could soon tell. These lines of light went out toward the earth and Harry then thought they were to *send messages* to those whom the spirits wish to reach on earth. You know sometimes you see men putting up poles and wires along the streets, do you know what they are for? ("Yes, telegraph wires.") Yes, they are telegraph wires, they send messages to and fro on earth by these wires. You cannot see the messages? Well, you cannot see these spirit wires, but they are here all the same, and Harry was soon busy sending a line of light or a wire toward his mother. If she could only see him do it. Every grand truth comes to earth on those angel wires, Harry would think, and then his wire would grow.

The next time I will tell you about—which island would you prefer?

Answer—"The Island of Pearl."

CHAPTER III.

THE LAST time, we visited "The Island of Light," (meaning the place
of perfect Truth); to-day we are to
go with Harry to the "Island of
Pearls."

Twelve children, including Harry,
were to visit the Island of Pearls.
Two beautiful angels, one wearing a crown of
pearls, the other with a crown of pure light, were
to accompany them. Also each child had a par-
ticular guardian or teacher to explain what
they saw.

The boats or canoes in which they were to
go, were made of pearl. Some were snowy
white, others were iridescent, (many colors;)
these boats represent pure and joyous thoughts.

Harry noticed the last time when he went to the
"Island of Light," through the "Rainbow Arch,"
that many other arch-ways, all leading into the
"Rainbow Arch," were passed. This time they
entered one of these side arch-ways, under an
arch-way of Lilies, and passing swiftly over
the clear water, they soon saw a beautiful island, with many colored lights, radiating from

it. Along the shore were beautiful shells, and
pearls. The shells were lined with rose-color
and gold, and as many of you have often heard
a sound from the sea-shell like the sound of
the ocean, so there came sweet music from the
shells along the shore, and even the light with
its pearly tints made music too. The two
Angels, one of Truth and one of Purity, who
preceded them, welcomed all the children to
the island. The Angel of Purity, with beautiful white face and a crown of Pearls, passed on
to a white terrace in the center of the Island,
but the children each were led into separate
paths by the teachers, and had to find their
way by various means.

Harry heard one little boy crying; his name
was Georgie when he lived on the earth, and
hastening to him he asked what he was weeping for? Georgie pointed to the path before
him. "See! there are black pearls?, and I cannot pass." But why can you not? and what
are black pearls?" Georgie said: "I don't
know, only when I look at them I remembered once when I was on earth I was very angry, and struck my sister and cried because I
was angry, and mother asked me if I was sorry,
and I said "no." Now when I see those black
pearls I think of that time, and I cannot go
any farther to see the beautiful lady. "Never
mind," said Harry, very kindly, we will wait
too. Georgie knelt down on the path and

and wept, and thought he would like to ask
his mother and little sister to forgive that
naughty boy.   When he looked up his teacher was smiling; the pearls had changed to
a white color, but he only wept again and felt
so unworthy to be in that lovely place.   Then
when he finally turned to go back, he saw the
teacher beckoning him to come on, for the
pearls were all washed white now.   How were
they made white? (Ans. Because he was
sorry!) Yes, his tears were penitent tears,
and they made the pearls white.

Harry went on his pathway and laughed
when he saw some pearls of the bright colors,
red, golden and blue; then he remembered
how once his mother had gone away from
home a long time, and when she came back
he was so glad to see her that he wept for
joy.   These pearls were tears of joy, and love,
but all found many lovely things in their paths;
pearls that shaped themselves with flowers;
like tears of childhood; some could not go
more than half the way along the path that led
to where the Angel of Purity stood.   They
found some selfish thought, some unworthy
deed stopped the way, but every little tear
shed in sympathy for others made a bright
pearl along their paths or a white flower.   They
saw before long that none could reach the
beautiful white pavilion or temple where the
"Angel of Purity" stood, except those who had

no selfish thought, no sorrow for their own wrong.

How many of those little children reach the temple and the Angel of Purity? Do you think any were absolutely free from selfishness? Some came very near, almost to the entrance, but all have to turn back and come by another way.

I will tell you *that way* by and by.

The next time where shall we go? (Ans. to the "Island of Roses.") Yes, Harry has been there, we will go?

CPAPTER IV.

THE ISLAND OF ROSES.

THE LAST time we went with Harry to the "Island of Pearls," and before that to the "Island of Light;" on each of these delightful journeys Harry and his companions passed *under* and through the "Rainbow Arch." Yes it is made of tears of sympathy, and sympathy is the result of kindness, and kindness is akin to love.

To-day we do not take little canoes or boats, but we pass along a pathway beautifully bordered with flowers. This pathway leads *over* the "Rainbow Arch," and is broader and more beautiful as we pass on. The flowers by the wayside are lovely, but you see them every day in summer. They are daisies, buttercups, violets, pinks and all home-like flowers. These are formed of "little deeds of kindness." If you share something that you have with a play-mate, that makes a daisy; if you help a play-mate who falls and gets hurt, instead of run-ning away, that makes a pink. So all along the way leading to the "Island of Roses," are these flowers of *"daily deeds of kindness."*

Harry and his companions were preceded by a beautiful angel, whose face was as pure as white roses; whose lips were like the red rose and who wore a crown of roses. As we come near the entrance, the odor of many roses floats out to meet us, and fair faces peep from among the buds and flowers; these are sweet children who went from earth-life and are "rosebuds" now. We enter the "Island of Roses" by a gate-way formed of roses in every variety of color. An inscription is over the gate-way; it is the *eleventh commandment* (can any of you in the class tell me what *is* the eleventh com-mandment? No? well, I will not tell you now but will wait until next time and expect you to tell me.) Passing under and through the gate-way they found themselves each in beautiful gardens of roses, but ah! some had thorns; can

you tell what were the thorns? One little boy
felt a thorn pierce his foot and then he remembered that he loved his playmates, but *one* he
loved because he brought him nice presents;
and he feared that he would not have loved
him so well if he could not have brought the
gifts. You are told to love your parents, why?
(Ans.—Because they love us.) Yes, but if they,
do not love you must you love them still? (Yes)
Well, these gardens where there are thorns
with the roses are made of such love as most
children and people have—you love those who
love you—you are kind to those who are kind
to you; you love your parents because you are
hungry and they feed you, you need clothing
and they give it. But whom are you to love
regardless of all this? (Ans.—We must love
everybody.) Yes, you must love everybody.

Harry soon found himself before another
gate-way, more beautiful than the first; it
seemed to open to a fairer portion of the isl-
and and there were buds of white roses at the
entrance. Over the pathway, in pure white
and golden roses, were inscribed the words of
"The Golden Rule." Can any one repeat it?
("Do unto others as you would have others do
to you.") Yes, and another inscription in still
brighter and whiter roses—"Love Your Enemies." Harry passed by the gate-way and his
companions were behind him; they had found
each some briar or thorn of selfishness, to bar

their way.   Harry found *his* brier here, for he
remembered a teacher who was unkind to him
and had punished him without cause.   Harry
had always been a loving boy.   He had loved
his mother and friends, and not only those
who loved him, but the poor and friendless,
but he had hated that teacher and had resolved that when he grew to be a man, he
would "get even with him some way."   Now,
when he stood before that gate-way, he felt
ashamed of that thought, and there came up a
spirit of forgiveness, he wished he could see
that teacher and forgive him: he drew nearer
the gate-way and still thought how much he
would like to do him a kindness; yes, he would
give him a flower from his garden!   Harry
was inside the gate-way, where the roses had
no thorns.   Along the beautiful way were bor-
ders of roses, and far away, yet ever coming
nearer, was a beautiful face and form, with a
crown of light and robes of brightness; the
angel crowned with roses took Harry nearer
and it was HE, the one who said "Suffer little
children to come unto me;" do you know who
said that? (Ans.—Jesus.)   Yes.   Why was
Jesus great and why did Harry see Him in the
fairest part of the Island of Roses?   Was he
a great soldier?   (No.)   Was he great in
learning?   (No.)   In what was he great?   (In
love.)   Yes, He was greatest of all in love.   So

the "Island of Roses" is the *Home of Pure Love*."

Do not forget to tell me next time what is the eleventh commandment. We will go further on in the "Island of Roses" next time.

CHAPTER V.

THE ISLAND OF ROSES.

(Continued.)

IS ANY one in the class prepared to tell me the eleventh commandment. Ans. Love one another. Yes. "A new commandment I give unto you: that you love one another."

Who gave this commandment? Ans. Jesus.

Where did we go last Sunday? Ans. – To the Island of Roses.

What *is* the Island of Roses? Ans.—The Island of Love.

What are the thorns? Ans.—Selfishness.

What inscription was over the inner gateway? Ans.—The Golden Rule.

What *other* message was there? Ans.—Love your enemies.

Then Harry learned, as we all must learn, not only to love those who love us, but to love those who do not love us, and last and best of all, to love those who seek to do us injury.

Whom did we see within the inner gateway? Ans.—Rosebuds.

Who are the Rosebuds? Ans.—Little children.

Whom did we see blessing them? Ans.—Jesus.

Yes. Why did he bless them? (a pause) Because they are bad? Ans.—No, because they are good. Yes' when they are good they are blessed.

What did he say when he blessed them? Ans.—"Suffer little children to come unto me and forbid them not, for of such is the kingdom of heaven."

We are still in the Island of Roses. Harry was very, very happy, all he saw and felt made him think of his mother and long to tell her of the lovely things he had seen.

On the very day when Harry visited the "Island of Roses, his mother, still sorrowing for his love, went to the beautiful spot in the cemetery where his form had been laid, she

saw with unspeakable delight, a *Rose* blooming over the grave.

She did not remember having planted a Rose
and it seemed to her Harry must himself have
planted it there. It gave her comfort to think
so, and in one sense it was true, for there is an
old proverb that says "when flowers bloom
over a grave they are angel's smiles from paradise," and do you know *the spirits* of the flowers must come from heaven, and may be the
thoughts of little children in heaven become
flowers when they reach the earth:

Harry's mother felt happier than she had
since her boy was borne away to the other
world, and looking up she thought she saw
Harry's face above her, surrounded by a bright
light. She was not mistaken, although she did
not see him with her external vision (any more
than you can see the air) still there is a finer
sight of which I have told you, and she saw
him: He left with her a lovely white Rose
that he had gathered near the Master's feet,
and every morning and evening, at her hymns,
or work, or prayers, Harry's mother *felt* his
presence.

He also visited others who were in sorrow,
and even found out his former teacher, the one
who had been unkind, and, seeing him in
trouble, Harry was not glad, but full of pity,
and placing his hand upon the aching head of
the teacher, the latter soon fell asleep, and

dreamed a lovely dream. He thought he saw a beautiful boyish face and heard a lovely voice telling him to "take courage, the clouds will pass away," and he saw many garlands of beautiful flowers, a· d felt their cool dews upon his brow; nor was it a dream, for Harry was there.

We now pass on to a very lowly gate-way, and Harry observed all who entered were obliged to kneel or bend the head, but beyond it were beautiful white lilies of the valley, with waxen bells, and large snowy lilies, and over the gate-way was an inscription about the pure of heart.

What is this gate-way? is it the gate way of *pride* of goodness? (a pause), one child answers—"The gate of humility.". Yes, it is the gate-way of humility, for all who do *good* with *loving* hearts are humble and do not boast of their good deeds. This gate-way leads to the Island of Lilies.

CHAPTER VI.

ISLAND OF LILIES.

UINA.—"Where do we go to-day?"
CHILDREN.—"To the Island of Lilies."
O.—"Through what gate-way do we
pass to get to the Island of Lilies?"
C.—"(after a pause) "The gate of
Humility."

O—"Is this a lofty gate-way?"

C.—"No, it is lowly."

O—Yes, it means that when we have perfect love we are also full of humility, and then
we are ready to pass to the Island of Lilies—
What inscription about the "pure in heart" did
I tell you we would find?

C—"Blessed are the pure in heart for they
shall see God."

O—Does this mean that God is a man and
that we shall see him with our mortal eyes?

C—"No, it means with our spirits."

O—Does it mean we shall see him as we
see each other?"

C—No, it means feel."

O—Yes, it means *perceive, or feel in spirit,*

for Jesus said, and we all know 'God is a spirit.' "

Harry saw the lowly arch-way, and the inscription, and wondered what it meant, for he knew he had passed from earth and felt he was in Heaven, but he had not *seen* God, then the true meaning dawned upon him, that all who are good, and pure and loving *see* God, for He is within them, and Harry was filled with a wonderful joy, he longed to tell his mother that he had *seen* or *perceived* God, the all pervading, loving presence. Harry then passed through the lovely gate-way, his heart full of love and joy. The vision that met his spirit was indeed beautiful! Every tree and flower, and Temple and Pavilion, was formed of white flowers, many of them lilies, and all were full of fragrance, and out of the lilies came a sound as of music like your voices, singing "Blessed are the pure in heart for they shall see God."

A lovely spirit child came and stood beside him, bearing a crown of white Lilies, and Harry knew it was a spirit sister, who went away from earth before he came to know her. They both passed, with one desire to the mother who was looking at Harry's portrait in her room on earth. She was no longer sorrowful as she was when Harry first went away, for she had many times seen his spirit and felt his presence, now the brother and sister pressed close to her side and placed the crown of

lilies on her brow, she smiled, and her eyes
filled with tears of gratitude, for she felt their
presence, and saw them standing there, she
gave thanks to the "Giver of all," for the blessing of spirit sight that had changed her sorrow into joy.

When Harry returned with his sister to the
Island of Lilies, he found that many of those
white blossoms had unfolded in his absence,
and then, he set to work to perform some deed
of pure love and kindness. Each day a snowy
lily was placed on his mother's heart, and each
hour some new work of love engaged his attention. There too, in the Island of Lilies he
saw the Great Teacher who said when on earth,
"Blessed are the pure in heart, for they shall
see God." The next time we will visit the
Island of Violets.

A SONG OF LILIES.

———

BLESSED are the pure in heart"
  Little children come and sing.
You can purity impart.
    Perfect joy and love ye bring.
      "What in the heart of the lily hides?"
      Purity— there God abides.

Blessed are the pure in heart."
  Unselfish in life and deed.
Suffering from slanders' dart.
    Pitiful in time of need.
      What the lilies sing to you
      Is purity—God dwells with you.

"Blessed are the pure in heart."
  Chime on lilies over head
Or in lowly garden bed.
    Where so e'er your petals start.
      For I hear you ever say
      "God is with the pure alway."

Crown him lilies pure and white.
  Crown him blossoms bright and fair.
Messenger of love and light.
    Breathing Love's breath everywhere.
      He who lowly here hath trod.
      Pure in heart, and seeing God.

CHAPTER VII.

THE ISLAND OF VIOLETS.

ARRY passed over a small foot-bridge formed of blue, leading from the Island of Lilies. There were blue waves of light all around, and a blue ether enveloped this fair Island, at the farther end of the bridge was an inscription, which read;

"HE VISITETH THE LOWLY."

"BY YOUR WORTH YE ARE EXALTED"

Through the gate-way of Humility leading down into a lovely glen, this bridge at last led Harry to the "Island of Violets." Never, in all the woody dells, or on all the mossy banks of earth, has there bloomed so many violets as met Harry's vision. A sweet girl with soft blue eyes came forward to meet him, and many smiling faces greeted him, modestly, yet full of joy. He heard a sound of soft music from all the beautiful dells where the violets grew, and the words that greeted him sounded familiar—

"Little deeds of kindness, little words of love,
Make the earth an Eden, like the world above."

Now he realized what it meant, for every

violet he saw blooming there—white violets, like a maidens' heart; yellow violets, like joys of childhood; blue violets, like the truth and love of the lowly—all these were the result of loving deeds. How beautiful they seemed! Many lowly acts unrecorded except by the angel of light, were here written in fragrant flowers. Harry modestly blushed when he saw a bed of exquisite blue violets in which his own name appeared, and another name was linked with his. The incident commemorated by this lovely bed of blossoms had almost faded from his memory, but it was a "little deed of kindness." Harry was going to school one warm spring day when on earth, and he passed the cot of a poor woman who had a little girl, Mary, she also attended the same school. When he arrived at the path leading to the gate, Mary came running out going to school also, Harry said "good morning," and pleasantly chatted with Mary as they walked along, presently he looked up, saying, "you've forgotten your lunch." Mary's face flushed in an instant, and she could not reply, but Harry quickly read the cause, her mother had nothing to give her child for lunch. Harry formed a quick resolution and hastily put it in practice, he set his basket down in front of Mary, saying, "you must take mine, I shall not miss it, and every day I will bring yours in one basket and mine in another, so they will not tease you." He fulfilled his word, and now, in this lovely, lovely place, *his* violets were waiting for him.

--- -- ----- -

SONG OF THE VIOLETS.

LOWLY, lowly, we are but small,
But our blossoms are true,
White violets for *modesty*,
Gracious deeds are the blue,
Little the work we can do,
But let the heavens shine through.

Maidens, fair as white violets,
Little deeds answer for all,
For the true heart never forgets:
Larger deeds grow from the small,
Sweet words, loving deeds are bright,
Ye bring sweetest delight.

Violets golden ye are bright gems,
Sweet deeds of childish grace,
Fit for angel's diadems,
Filling your holy place,
Laughing yet loving all the while,
Violets how ye do smile!

Blue violets, the love of the soul,
Modesty, truth and pure worth,
How the the heavens their leaves unroll,
Bringing their treasures to earth,
Blue eyes windows of heaven's light,
Lend us your purest sight.
The next time we will visit the "Lilies of the Valley."

CHAPTER VIII.

THE LILIES OF THE VALLEY.

ON THE Island of Lilies, apart from the avenues of light that lead to the White Temple of Purity, Harry and his sister saw a small, narrow pathway leading down into a beautiful vale; this pathway was bordered with plain, home-like flowers, and even lowly plants that many pass unnoticed. There were cool, shaded grottoes beside the way, and from these came whispered sounds like spirits in prayer. Pure, pale spirits with dove like eyes, smiled sweetly upon them as they passed, but never left their lowly occupations. Some were bending above the suffering, rejected ones of earth. who from poverty and want had passed to the immortal world. Pale white waxen bells of the lilies of the valley bloomed everywhere, their exquisite fragrance made sweet music, and the sound that came was, "Blessed are the meek " No thought of pride. no vain boasting of holiness or goodness, ever entered there, and these pure spirits, clad in snowy whiteness, were intent on ministering to the lowly ones of earth.

Harry felt himself humbled in the presence of such gentleness and purity, and saw them doing such good works all unconsciously, that he almost felt he had been good only to be praised. There he found no self-consciousness, no pride of goodness, no thought other than purest charity. Those scorned on earth were here relieved with tender care. Those rejected sinful ones whom men despised, were taken and made clean, washed of impure thought in the clear waters of Truth, and made to feel that they, too, were immortal.

Harry and his sister saw a large company of spirits, clad in white, singing a sweet song over a new born soul lately received from earth, they sang:

LOWLY. lowly. enter into rest.
  Love is pure and holy.
  Heaven is here expressed:
    Ye who pine and languish.
  Ye who sin below,
    Leave your pain and anguish.
  Here loves' fountains flow.

Lowly, lowly, good deeds hid from sight,
  Enter pure and holy
Into perfect light,
    What on earth is hidden,
    Here shall be revealed.
Hatred is forbidden,
    Love is unconcealed.

Lowly, lowly, peace and rest are here,
    Darkness passeth slowly
But the day is near:
    O, ye weary, waiting
Come and be at rest.
    Earth is oft belating
Turn to Heaven's breast.

Lowly, lowly, good deeds out of sight,
    Thoughts all pure and holy
Here shall greet the sight
    Incense of the spirit
Rises up in prayer,
    Meekness shall inherit
All things unaware.

LILIES OF THE VALLEY.

SWEETEST chiming of waxen bells,
In the lowliest shadiest dells,
What is this you sing to me?
    "Humility."

Fragrant breath of woodland moss,
With your sweet odors stealing across,
What message can you bring to me?
    "Humility."

Heart of love, for love's own sake,
Doing good tho' all forsake,
What is the *best* thing here for me?
    "Humility."

All ye lowliest holiest things,
By lifes' cool and sequestered springs,
What can the secret of loving be?
    "Humility." -

ROSE BUDS.

LIPS LIKE rose buds what do you say,
Chattering, lisping all the long day?
      "I love ou, mamma, I love ou."

Thoughts like rose buds, what do you think?
All the day long of food and drink?
      "I love ou, mamma, I love ou."

By and by the roses will grow,
Cheeks and lips and heart will o'erflow.
Who will you love then?   No one can know.

APRIL SHOWERS FOR MY FLOWERS.

TEARS of pity refresh the desponding heart.
   Tears of sympathy comfort the sad.
   Tears of joy are the dews of love.

Rain drops are to the buds and grass like
little deeds of kindnes to the weary heart.

Do not be afraid of the rain; it brightens the
flowers and will not harm you-- but

Do not wear wet garments, that is like clinging to a sorrow in memory, when the lesson of it is past.

Tears of repentance make a rainbow gateway to Paradise.

Tears of sympathy and compassion build the arch-ways to the approach of heaven

Tears shed for another's woes, moisten the lilies in the gardens of paradise.

LITTLE MISS SNOW DROP AND MISS SWEET BRIAR.

A STORY IN VERSE.

PART I.

IN a beautiful palace Miss Snow Drop dwelt,
 Surrounded by jewels and glittering gems;
At her feet a wooing the lovers all knelt
 To offer their bright diadems.

The palace was fashioned around and above
 With pearls and with diamonds of light,
And where-so-ever Miss Snow Drop might move
 Her eyes, there were frost blossoms white.

But Miss Snow Drop was beautiful and cold,
 And no butterfly on his bright quest
Ever rested a-near her a sweet talk to hold,
 And no humming bird came there to rest.

She hoarded her beauty against the bright sun
    Till she like the snow was as white;
She never let tears down her fair cheeks run,
    So her eyes were unwashed by their light.

The birds and the honey bees stayed far away'
    And Miss Snow Drop declared she was glad—
For insects and birds she detested alway,
    And indeed they were all very bad.

As for Violets, Daisies and such common trash,
    "Who would ever stoop down to see them?'
Miss Snow Drop would one of her bright jewels flash,
    And all would hasten to her garment's hem.

One day at her feet a poor, sweet violet,
    [Beguiled by the spring's early kiss]
With blossoms all chilled and leaves all bewet,
    Asked shelter of that stately miss.

And what do you think? Miss Snow Drop turned pale,
    Not with sympathy but with great pride,
Saying: "Seek for your spring-time; why should it fail?
    'Twas better for you if you died."

But of all the flowers that summer loves best,
    Whether lilies her hatred inspire,
Or roses, or pansies, or all of the rest,
    She most could not bear the "Sweet Brier."

" 'Twas so thorny and hateful, the horrible thing,
    And its blossoms were just fit to die,
And every butterfly rested its wing'
    And no humming bird ever went by—"

So the beautiful Snow Drop grew colder each day,
    Wrapped in splendor withdrew to her home.

Next time I will tell how her life passed away,
How a foe to the palace did come.

— . —. .

PART II.

NOW Miss Sweet Briar's home was sunny and bright,
    Open wide to the spring time air;
And open to every blest ray of light,
    To all mated birdies so fair—
For a hedge of green, protected by thorns,
    Made a shelter for nest of their young;
And the beautiful bloom that the Sweet Briar adorns,
    Made a perfume like soft censors swung.

One day a rude serpent attempted to steal
    The young in a nest near Sweet Briar,
But her bayonets bristled like finely wrought steel,
    And defeated the serpent's desire.

But a humming bird flew there to gather the food,
    For his gentle mate in the far nest,
And Sweet Briar gave him the honey-dew good,
    That she evermore held in her breast.

Sweet Briar was beloved by zephyrs and breeze,
    By sunlight, and dewdrop, and rain;
Because all her sweetness she gave forth to please,
    And they brought it all to her again.

But no rude hand could come near her fair home,
    For girded with an armor was she;
But gentle hearts knew by what pathway to come,
    To them was her home ever free.

Some blamed her for thorns that pierced the hand,
    But ne'er injured a butterfly's wing;

She always replied, "love can ever command
    I harm none who no violence bring.

Until beauty is safe and no serpents are near,
    God gives us protection the while;
But loving ones know and approach without fear,
    For they see my welcoming smile.

My temple is open to all lovely things,
    To bird, breeze, and bright butterfly;
To honey bee busy, and humming bird's wings,
    And to maidenhood's bright happy eye.

"A little while yet and the blossoms are gone,
    But fragrance still filleth my leaves;
And all spring and summer the hedge sparrow's tone
    Is heard; and the bright golden sheaves

Are filled with my odor, the silver moonlight
    Loves me and this fragrance of mine,
And the Nightingale sings to me in the still night,
    Of beauty and rapture divine.

PART III.

ONE day as Miss Snow Drop was resting awhile
    [For she rested, but slept not in a cold icy bed]
She awoke with a start, for she thought that she saw
    A huge monster approaching her white snowy bed.

He came nearer and nearer and covered the door,
    With chains made of silver or glittering steal,
Weaving as he came all her bright arbor o'er
    With chain upon chain all her home to conceal.

Too frightened to scream, in her palace alone,
    Miss Snow Drop beheld that her prison was made;

She could utter no word, nor a sigh, nor a tone,
  And a sense of deep horror her heart did pervade,

Not a friend in the wide world, no bird in the air,
  Nor insect to frighten the monster away;
O would she had comforted violet fair,
  For perhaps some of her friends might happen that way.

Round and round as a wheel was the soft netting spread,
  Over, under and through all her palace of white;
And the grim monster sat in the center not dead,
But keeping close watch, full in Miss Snowdrop's sight.

Day by day, night by night went the life from her heart,
  The cold heart, the selfish the unloving soul;
Until when the last breath of her bloom did depart,
  The monster wound up all his chains in a roll

Leaving Miss Snowdrop dead, and her palace once white,
  All faded and stained with his poisonous breath;
And no one lamented for Miss Snow Drop's light,
  For every one knew she was selfish; at death

Of Miss Snow Drop, the monster sought pretty Sweet Briar
  And wove o'er her arbor his glittering chains;
She fluttered and scolded and said in her ire,
  "Wait awhile you will have nothing here for your pains."

So he wove and she waited till far in the sky
  The sun god arose in his palace of gold;
And Sweet Briar fluttered her banner on high
  The banner of bloom and of beauty untold.

When swift from the woodland the humming bird flew,
  To gather the honey-dew for his loved mate;
Sweet Briar was the first to attract his swift view,
  And his bright pinions fluttered with pleasure elate.

"Come this way," said Sweet Briar nodding her head,
  And the humming bird answering straightway her call;

Fluttered close by the monster upsetting his bed,
  And breaking his chains and his prison bars all.

For the monster was only a spider, who wove
  His cobweb to catch any poor harmless fly;
And pretty Miss Sweet Briar knew that the love
  Of the bird and the bee, would not let them pass by

When her home or her bloom were in danger so near,
  We perceive that Miss Snow Drop was frightened to death:
Because of her selfishness was her life drear,
  While pretty Miss Sweet Briar, with every breath

Gave blessings to others and they in return,
  Blessed her and protected, thus love begets love,
And even the spider her pity did move,
  For he could not help being so cruel; so spurn

Not, nor scorn not, nor fear not, Sweet Briar,
  For your love and your generous nature will last,
While cold selfish hearts like Miss Snow Drop's expire,
  And through fear all their beauty is vanquished at last.

Pride and selfishness are like Miss Snow Drop you know,
  Love and generous thoughts are like wayward Sweet Briar;
And better have love than the wintery glow,
  That sparkles but gives naught that can kindness inspire.

LILIES FROM THE GARDEN OF GOD.

CONSIDER the lilies how they grow; they toil not neither do they spin, and yet I say unto you that Solomon in all his glory was not arrayed like one of these"

Pure thoughts are the lilies in the garden of a pure heart.

Make your spirit pure and deeds, words and thoughts will yield white blossoms.

Perfect purity is perfect love.

"To the pure all things are pure."

Unconscious as a lily in bloom, is the heart of pure maidenhood.

White like lilies of the valley, are the thoughts of mamma's darling.

If you would always be pure—be loving, be truthful, be charitable, be just.

LILY.

[A Recitation.]

———

LILY'S brow is white as snow,
　　Because of the white thoughts within;
Lily's hands more warmly glow,
　　Because her heart is free from sin.

Lily's cheek is often pale,
　　Not with anger, but with pain:
But her spirit does not quail,
　　Soon she gently smiles again.

Lily's hair is burnished gold,
　　Like the sunshine of her smile;
Lily has great wealth untold,
　　But she gives it all the while.

———

MY GARDEN.

———

I HAVE a little garden to plant here on the earth;
　It is a bright and sunny spot, fit for the seeds of
　　worth.

Just here close to the woodland, I plant my violets;
With ferns and mosses near them, where the dew their
　faces wet,
For violets are modesty, and shrink from glare of day,
But trusting look to heaven, blue as the sky alway.

And here I plant my pansies, with baby faces bright
To laugh away all sorrow, and bring the heart delight:
For pansies are for heart's ease. and sooth the weary here.
So there beside the pathway I place. to have them near.

My lilies of the valley. within this sheltered nook
I plant. but their sweet fragrance will make you pause
 and look;
Their snowy wax-bells glisten in sweet simplicity.
But this is what they tell you. "Trust and humility."

My roses must be planted here before the eyes of all.
Rose buds and blooming roses—each path and garden
 wall
Must be adorned with roses. around us and above.
For our roses have no thorns. and their language is all
 Love.

My daisies I will plant here upon the meadows fair.
And all along the pathway. they must grow everywhere;
For daisies are white star beams. from heaven fair and
 bright.
And they always mean gladness. they bring us pure de-
 light.

My lilies they best grow here a little way along:
Sheltered by these young poplars. from the rude wind
 so strong;
For lilies speak of purity. and should sequestered be:
Sensitive is the poplar, a guard for purity.

My buttercups I'll scatter upon the garden grass.
Wherever you may wander they greet you as you pass:
For they are like bright thoughts, scattered from worlds
 above,
I place them here for brightness, along your way to
 move.

And here I place tube roses. within this sunny bed.

For their beauty and fragrance must meet us where we
  tread:
One blossom fills the whole room with perfume and
  with light:
Tube roses are loving thoughts and loving deeds so bright.

And here upon this streamlet the water lily blooms,
With roots down in the darkness, but upward through
  the gloom
The sunlight soft has won it, the sky protects above,
It teaches Inspiration, and guidance from above.

I have within my garden, many more flowers bright,
And to adorn my grottoes, are jewels of pure light:
And trees that grow in beauty, and birds with splendid
  wing,
And lovely songs of gladness these birds forever sing.

Some other day I'll tell you more names of my sweet
  flowers,
And bring you to my grottoes, to rest within my bowers:
If you will bring a blossom to add unto my joys,
For the flowers are your sweet thoughts, My Garden,
  girls and boys.

MY FLOWER GARDEN.

T THE "Children's hour" each Sunday we plant and water the flowers. We always have a little prayer, something like this: I say a line and the children all repeat it after me ,then I say another, and so on to the end:

FATHER thy little children come
    With thanks and praises unto thee:
Receive our gifts within thy home
    And make our spirits glad and free.

We bless thee for the morning light.
    We bless thee for the noon-tide ray:
May we each, as the morn grows bright.
    See love and wisdom day by day.

We bless thee for the evening hour.
    When heaven is near and stars come forth,
O'er death's twilight give us power
    To see the realm of spirit birth.

May all our footsteps guided be,
    Our hearts be pure, from strife and sin.
And may we show our love of thee
    By loving thoughts and deeds—*Amen.*

BIRD TALK.

CHEEP, cheep, cheep, cheep.
Little sparrows, peep and cheep;
    T-whit, te-whit-so sweet.
Red breasted robin—So sweet;
    T-rill, te-rill, te-te-te-rill.
Little ground thrush, so still;
Jenny wren, jenny wren, are you here?
What a bustle, good morning my dear.

    Trill, peek, tat, tat-a-tat, a-tat.
Such a gay wood cock, a red hat.
A black bird, as sure as can be;
    Bobolink, spink, spunk, spee,
    Te-rol-e, te-rol-e, te-rol-e.
How happy we birds can all be!

DEWDROPS FOR MY FLOWERS.

BABY'S tears are like dew drops, the sun kisses the flowers till the dew drops are dry; so mamma kisses the eyes and cheeks of baby, and smiles come again.

Tears are sometimes the only mirror in which heaven is seen. Looking earth-

ward the clear sky is reflected in the raindrops;
so tears reflect the joy overhead.

Loving thoughts and deeds are like dew
upon the flower—refreshing.

Dry your tears quickly, if they are selfish
ones, that they may better see the sunshine.

Tears of sympathy are not like those of sorrow, the former brightens the spirit, the latter
corrodes.

Dew drops for the lily, storms for the oak;
to the sensitive be gentle, to all be kind.

RECITATION FOR BABY.

LITTLE bright eyes to see the light,
Little soft hands dimpled and white;
Little round ears to hear the birds sing,
Lips, mamma says, like roses in spring;
Little head plotting more mischief each day
Little feet running every way.
Now if you think there's more I can do,
Wait, if you please till I grow big as you.

SUNBEAMS FOR MY FLOWERS.

Y OU CANNOT smile too often. Gladness is the sunshine of life.

Baby's tears are April showers. Baby's smiles are mamma's sunbeams; baby's happiness is mamma's joy.

The laughter of children is like the chiming of golden bells.

SUNBEAMS.

A RECITATION FOR LITTLE FOUR YEAR OLD.

S EE THE sunbeams on the flowers,
  Dancing brightly all the day:
Peeping through the baby bowers,
  Having many things to say.

See the sunbeams on the stream,
  Glancing, dancing, ever bright:
See the lake, where e'er they gleam,
  Grow like heaven's golden light.

See them shine on sister's hair,
  Turning every thread to gold;
See them smiling everywhere,
  Sunbeams, I am four years old.

Don't you see them in my eyes?
  Mamma does, they're love you know;
I wish I had some butterflies,
  Sunbeams, tell me where they grow?

— — —

SEE HOW many hearts you can make glad every day; then at night you can say to the angels, I have sunbeams enough to make a little piece of heaven's day.

When baby smiles in his sleep, an angel kisses him. When you smile on those who are sad, the angels open the door of heaven and let the sunbeams through.

Don't be afraid to be glad. As the mists and cobwebs fade before the sunbeams of morning, so sadness flies.

Laughter is kindness, but mocking derision is a shadow.

The smiles of angels are tender as morning twilight.

FLOWERS FROM MY GARDEN.

KIND deeds are like blossoms blown by the summer wind. They bring sweet fragrance, and their fruitage is love.

A kind word may sooth a saddened heart: a kind act heal it.

Love is better than duty; duty binds for a day or a year, but love binds forever.

"Love one another." This is the Queen of all the Flowers.

With this our garden is full, for we have Charity—Mercy—Kindness—all good thoughts and deeds by loving one another.

Charity is a starry flower, one of the children of Love.

Mercy is a fragrant blossom and the sister of Charity.

Kindness is also like these, and is the child of Love.

"Be kind to your brothers and sisters."

"Be kind to your mates."

' Obey (love) your parents."

"Kind words can never die."

"Blessed are the merciful."

"Love conquers all fear."

"Love is stronger than faith."
"Charity suffereth long and is kind."
"Charity covereth many sins."
"Charity never faileth."
"Love is the fulfilling of the law."

These form a floral wreath whose golden and white links are love.

DIAMOND DROPS.

RUTH is the diamond of the soul, as its pearl is purity and its ruby love, while the topaz is knowledge, and the sapphire wisdom.

Be truthful, and like the clear diamond shall your light shine.

As a clear beam of white light, unbroken by clouds, such is the ray of truth.

One truth can illume the whole world, but a thousand errors can only shadow a little corner.

Darkness cannot radiate but light can. So error and evil fall back on the heart that sends them forth, but love and truth brighten a hundred thousand lives.

Into the prison the ray of light may pass, but the depths of darkness cannot reach beyond the shadow of the prison wall.

MY FLOWER GARDEN.

THIS is the planting time, is the soil ready?

The Spirit is the soil, and it should be free from stubble and thorns.

Are the seeds ready?

The seeds are good thoughts and knowledge, loving words and deeds.

Are the germs ready?

The germs are former seeds (thoughts), planted long ago, which are now to be transplanted.

How are they to be transplanted?

By having more room in your thoughts; more control over your lives.

Are the plants ready?

The plants are seeds already rooted, sprouted and grown, but which must be watered and carefully tended before the blossoms can come.

How are they watered?

By doing each day one's duty and letting the dews of kindness fall into one's life.

How are they tended?

By letting no thorns or briars grow; no weeds that would obstruct their growth, and by letting the sunshine of affection fall on them.

What are thorns, briars and weeds?

Angry thoughts or words, unkindness, untruthfulness. lack of charity.

QUESTIONS AND ANSWERS.

LITTLE BLUE EYES.

WHAT makes the trees, how do they grow?

TEACHER.

Each tree grows from a tiny shoot,
Each shoot is from a little seed.
There never could be trunk or root,
Nor branch, nor flower, nor leaf indeed,
Unless there were a *life within*,
A spirit, we call God, who gives
To every *seed* and *germ* its life,
And life to everything that lives.

"Why do the trees bear fruit?" (asks Tom.)

Because each thing that lives must be
Perpetual, and foliage comes
So that the seed may sheltered be.
We like the apples, and our homes
Are made more beautiful because
The fruit and trees give food and shade.
The fruit protects the seed these laws
Are wonderful, our God has made.

"How, is the world a "palace car?" (asks one.)

Who knows what is a palace car?
I see some of you know; ah well.
A *palace* is a dwelling bright,
In which the rich and favored dwell.
A *cottage* is humble and small
But may be pretty all the same;
A *hovel* is the worst of all,
And somebody must bear the blame.

A *palace car* is bright and fine,
  With windows large and cushioned seats,
And many polished pannels shine
  And many a pictured mirror greets
The eye: and springs are underneath,
  So that you never feel the jar
Or motion, 'tis as tho' a sheath
  Were placed around you— now a star
Like this world, may be very bright
  And beautiful if we but see
The lovely side—if our own sight
  Is freed from strife and misery,
But there are planets, brighter far
  And larger many times than ours,
And many a sun and many a star,
  That sparkles in the azure bowers,
Must be more beautiful than this,
  But if we do the best we can,
We *all* can have a home of bliss,
  And earth is a palace car for man.

"What are the stars?" (asks Rosy Cheeks,)

They all are worlds like ours, or suns
  Like that which gives our planet light,
Each one in its own orbit runs
  And far away beyond our sight
Are other suns and systems too,
  Moving like balls of light in space
Around some centre, to your view,
  They seem as points of light, they grace
The sky like flowers upon the grass,
  But they are worlds, governed by law
Of light and motion, and they pass
  In harmony, without a flaw
Through countless miles of space afar

In circling systems. full of life.
Each one a world, star after star,
With light and beauty ever rife.

OUINA'S FLOWER GARDEN.

A LETTER.

FRANKTOWN, Washoe Co., Nevada. Feb. 20, 1882.

DEAR OUINA:—

I have read your beautiful poem, "My Garden," in the
SPIRITUAL OFFERING; I like it very much. I have ever admired
your poems, but this one seems to let me speak to you. You write
us to come and see your "Grottoes," if we "will bring a blossom to
add to your joy;' this I surely would like to do, and think I have
several in my heart. I love the Indians, I love children, and I love
all humanity, so you can name my flower what you see it to be.
Perhaps, sometime in spirit, I can visit your garden.

    Yours in love and truth,   MATTIE J. AYLESWORTH.

OUINA'S ANSWER.

TO MATTIE.

DEAR Mattie, the spirit of your letter came
    While my Water Lily was far away.
So I could not answer nor give it a name,
    But I read it aloud to the children to-day.

But the thought of it long ago was sent.
    And planted among my flowers bright.
This letter is but an instrument
    To bring the answering buds to your sight.

You "love my poems"—that is a flower,
    Like an apple blossom, showing preference,

Appreciation—the bay leaf has power
  To tell of hidden poetic sense.

You "love the Indian"—a prarie flower.
  To tell of nature— a pine tree too,
That speaks of pity—the lonely dower
  Of the Red man. 'tis all that you can do.

You "love the children"—the innocents,
  The violets, daisies and buttercups bright:
The rose buds. all that have sweetest scents.
  A garden of flowers are the children. quite.

But the moss. that is as green velvet spread.
  Covering the ground with its tufts so bright,
Yielding caressingly where e'er you tread,
  Is "love ot children"—this brings delight.

But the love of Humanity is a great tree,
  That grows with all the strength of soul:
'Tis an oak. strong. sheltering and free,
  Seeking freedom and love's perfect goal.

For the high aspirations. and these you possess.
  I will give you a blossom full of love.
Not from the heart of the wilderness.
  But the "Mountain Pink"* blooming above.

*This is your spirit name. Ouina.

A MAY GREETING TO ANYBODY'S BABY.

CLAP your tiny hands ye leaves
  Baby buds and blossoms blow
Hither and thither, the earth weaves
  All your joy and gladness you know.

Little birds sing all your songs,
  For I am too full of joy to sing.
To you the art of music belongs,
  To you the flight of joyous wing.

But can you guess, you birds and flowers,
  Why I wish you to sing and bloom?
Angels have come to this world of ours,
  And ask everybody to give them room.

Little babies with dewy eyes,
  Welcome, welcome, to earthly bowers,
You give the children a glad surprise,
  For you brought from heaven all the flowers!

IMMORTALITY.

CHILD.

BUTTERFLY, butterfly, where did you grow?
  Are you a flower that blossomed with wings?
Such a rare creature earth seldom can show,
  Now here and there on each flower it swings.

BUTTERFLY.

No, I am not a flower or bird.
  I did not grow as the birds or the flowers.
But I awoke with never a word
  Out of a sleep, and came here to my bowers.

CHILD.

Butterfly, butterfly how did you sleep?
  What did you do before you could fly?
Such a strange secret you silently keep.
  Can any one solve it? Alas, can not I?

TEACHER.

The bright butterfly was a poor lowly worm.
  Creeping and crawling upon the ground.
But it wove a cocoon, or a web for its shroud,
  And died in that soft, silken covering wound.

Then, after a sleep, the shell burst, and lo,
  Wings and bright colors came forth in a day!
So, after the earth life and death here below.
  You live in a region of brightness alway.

Transformed as the butterfly, is the glad soul,
  Having cast off the garb as the worm on the earth,
With wings of bright thought it mounts to its goal.
  Glad and free, and most joyous in its heavenly birth.

DANDELIONS.

—·—

BABY saw the yellow blossoms, starry dandelions
  fair.
Baby plucked them to her bosom, pressed the yellow treasures rare.
Baby cried, "more fowers," 'more; eager were her
  eyes and hands.
Ever hastening before, snatching still the golden
  wands.

Many flowers still to gather, e'er the summer time
  is gone,
But in fair or stormy weather, dandelions still bloom
  on.
Baby's cheeks will bloom to roses, pearly teeth will
  pretty grow,
But no gold of earth discloses half the joy childhood
  can know.
Starry blossoms, baby loves you, and her eyes will
  ever greet
Like stars that bloom above you, while you shine at
  baby's feet.

FLOWERS FOR SEPTEMBER.

GOLDEN rod, Golden rod.
   Wave to me your yellow wand.
Bend and bow to me, and nod,
   Touch me with your velvet hand.

Asters wild, purple and gold
   In your chalices abound.
Richest tints and shades untold
   All along the way are found.

And beside the garden walk.
   Stately as fair maidens tall.
'Blooms the tinted Hollyhock:
   Climbing o'er that garden wall
Are the Morning Glories fair,
   Brightest flowers of a day.
And the white Petunias rare
   Tinting all the emerald way.

Marigolds, so bright and gay;
   Gladiolas, scarlet, red,
Pink and crimson, an array.
   Making glad the path we tread.

Autumn flowers are like life,
   Far more deep in tint and tone.
With life's golden beauty rife.
   Growing bright when day is done.

AN AUTUMN MEDLEY.

KATY-DID came out for a walk
  In the fair September night:
Mr. Grasshopper perched on a stalk.
Commenced to chatter and chatter and talk.
    Confusing Miss Katy-did quite.
    Katy-did, Katy-did, Katy-did."
  O, what did Miss Katy do?

The Locust espied her and set
  His rattle agoing at once.
And the Owl said "to-hoot, don't forget."
Miss Katy did flutter and fret.
    Because she had been such a dunce.
    "Katy-did, Katy-did, Katy-did,"
  O, what *will* Miss Katy do?

The Linnet sang low in the bush.
  The Cricket chirped merrily too.
  But what was Miss Katy to do
With such a great chatter and rush.
    Could she never escape from their view?
    "Katy-did, Katy-did, Katy-did."
  O, what *can* Miss Katy do?

Katy-did had a brother asleep.
When she stole out alone for a walk.
  And he heard all the chatter and talk,
And forth from his warm bed did creep.
    Then into their midst he did stalk.
"Katy-did "Katy-*didn't*."
    To hoot, tre-e-e-e-e to-te-le,
    "Tweet tweet" said the linnet.
"Katy-didn't"
    She didn't, She DIDN'T."
And all was still in a minute.

AUTUMN LEAVES.

HEAR them falling, falling, like a whisper of the dead,
Like memory's voices calling, paving the path we tread
With crimson hues and golden, like a mosaic olden.

Red sparkling from the maple, gold from the elm and
beech,
Pale yellow from the popple, varied as human speech,
As lightly falling on the ground, but unlike words they
never wound.

Blown by the warm west wind in brown-gold-crimson
clouds,
No stem nor tree can bind, ye go to weave your shrouds,
Play in the autumn sun and die, for your life work is done.

If we might thus like leaves grow brighter when death
comes,
Golden when like autumn sheaves to crown the earthly
home,
And then be caught away as leaves on a bright autumn
day.

And if leaving a trace like these along the track,
To cheer each coming face, and gaily looking back
Like a leaf blown on the air, ye could die and be as fair.

Whisper as gently too, and shine through golden mist,
As these sweet wand'rers do, by heavenly splendors kiss'd,
Then death indeed would be, loveliest of Sisters Three.*

*Birth, Earthly Love, and Death.

SEPTEMBER SUNSHINE.

ALL among the fading leaves
   See it shimmer,
All among the autumn sheaves
   See it glimmer;
Clear and bright, full of gold,
How much sunlight can the day hold?

Among the new grown meadows,
   Fields of new clover,
Chasing away the shadows,
   Under and over;
Sunset is round and red, the twilight gay
Melts as we tread into evening gray.

Over on the stream
   See it dance and gleam,
Gaily as in a dream
   It touches the spray;
Gold and red, red and gold,
How much color can the day hold?

On the purple clusters,
   On the peaches fair,
On the apples red and ripe,
   On the melons rare,
Purple, red, russet and gold,
How many colors can the day hold?

Dancing in the sunshine,
   Till day is done;
You little child of mine
   Have its gold won;
Crimson lips, laughing eyes, hair of gold,
All of life's sunshine one heart can hold.

A NOVEMBER CALL.

LITTLE bird belated
   Came to my cottage door.
"Oh, you so loving mated:
      Have you a place for more?
      It is late and I am weary.
      And the moor is cold and dreary."

Come in, come in little bird.
   There is room in our cottage small:
As soon as your voice I heard.
   I was waiting to ask you to call;
      Take some crumbs and some water too,
      And what else can I do?

"O, thank you, a moment to rest
   Then I must be up and away.
Far over the moor on a quest
      Of love, so I cannot long stay;
      Yes, a crumb and some water will do,
      But I hope I am not robbing you."

The next spring the days grew long,
   And the warm wind came up from the south,
We heard just the loveliest song.
   That ever came from a sweet bird's mouth
      Just outside the cottage door,
      Saying, "I've come back once more."

And there was the bird and his mate,
   Building their nest in our tree,
(The same bird that came so late)
      As happy as happy could be;
      And they filled the whole summer long
      With their beautiful, joyous song.

A crumb cast out in the cold,
  A word cast into the heart
That is sad, tho' 'tis never told.
  Will still make the giver glad:
    And good deeds like birds in the spring.
  Will return and evermore sing.

OUR LITTLE ROSY-TOES.

A STORY, TOLD BY CHATTERBOX.

CHAPTER I.

MAMMA had just put Rosy-toes to sleep and tucked her in the cradle, telling me (my name is Chatterbox) to rock the cradle gently, not to make any noise, and to let her know the moment Rosy-toes awoke.

Now, Rosy-toes was just the sweetest baby *you ever did see*, and I could hold her just as well as mamma, only they wouldn't let me—only *pretend* to let me hold her when papa or mamma or Annie had her. Pretty soon my arm got tired rocking the cradle; then I tried to rock it with my foot, but that made a noise and almost woke Rosy-toes, but I sung: "By o-baby, by-o-baby," and she went to sleep. Then the kitty came along and wanted to play with the tassel on my little chair tidy, and I wanted to play with kitty, so I took her up in my lap and said: "'S'sh, kitty, little Rosy-toes is asleep and you mustn't make any noise or mamma will scold;" but kitty kept on purring and p-u-r-r-ing until I thought she surely would waken Rosy-toes, then, all of a sudden, kitty gave a spring and jumped into the cradle, right on top of Rosy-toes. Kitty was gone in a second, but Rosy-toes screamed and cried, and I thought / could take her out of the cradle; so I tried, and lifted her most out, then she was too heavy, and I was so afraid, and let Rosy-toes fall. Then I was so scared I ran away as fast as I could go and hid under the lilac bush right by the side of kitty–– —

CHAPTER II.

HERE was I?   O,—well kitty and I kept just as still as mice, and never said a word, and Rosy-toes didn't make any noise either and I thought she was dead; then I heard mamma come rushing in and say: "O! my poor, darling baby;', and then I *did* hear Rosy-toes scream and scream, and scream, and hold her breath, and mammy talking to her all the while, and I cried too—softly at first because I didn't want mamma to hear, then louder and louder, for I thought she had forgotten poor little Chatterbox and never wanted to see me any more, just 'cause I had most killed Rosy-toes; and I only tried to lift her up to stop her crying.   Then I cried harder and harder, and wished Rosy-toes had never come to live with us, because mamma used to take me on her lap all the time; and now mamma never came at all, only sent Annie to tell me to "stop your noise naughty Chatterbox, for mamma is getting dear little Rosy-toes to sleep, and you will wake her, you bad girl."   Then Annie took hold of my little wrist and pulled me out from the lilac bush and said I must go to bed and not see my mamma any more that day—and I screamed just as loud as I could scream, and Annie took me around the back way, and up stairs, and put me to bed; but it wasn't near dark. Then kitty came to see what was the matter. and *I* think Rosy-toes is a very naughty baby to act so.

CHAPTER III.

I FORGOT all about Rosy-toes in the morning; mamma came into the room and kissed me, and said: "How is my little Chatterbox this bright morning?" And pretty soon Annie came in with Rosy-toes, all dressed in white, for a walk, (Rosy-toes can't walk but Annie carries her) and right on Rosy-toes' nose was a great big bump, and it made her look so funny, but she laughed at me, and I laughed, and I didn't ask mamma to send Rosy-toes away (for crying so for just a little bump), and I guess mamma thought she wouldn't speak to me about it for fear of hurting Rosy-toes' feelings; she was *real* good and I didn't say anything, only hung down my head, and mamma kissed me and said: "Mamma's little girl will never do so again?" I s'pose she meant Rosy-toes. Mamma is so good I

mean to forgive Rosy-toes, wouldn't you?
But I never took her out of the cradle again,
for I was afraid she would cry. Good-bye,
when I get through playing with my kitty I'll
tell some more about Rosy-toes and I, but
mamma says this story is long enough. Good-
bye.

A FAIRY STORY.

THREE fairies once lived in a cave near
the sea. Their mother (who was also a
fairy) lived in the world above, but
for some reason not known to them,
these three fairy children dwelt in this
cave. The tide came up twice every
twenty-four hours and stopped the entrance to the cave. There was no light of the
sun, nor moon, nor stars in the cave, but when
the three fairies were there the place was lighted as with many glittering lamps: and there
were jewels and bright flowers hung from pend-
ants over head.

The first of the three fairies was pale and
thoughtful, calm brow, and bright large eyes,
forever up-turned in prayer, and whenever the
tide was high, so that they could not pass out,
she would sit silently and quietly resigned

waiting, saying: "I can wait, it will not be long, the tide will surely go down."

The second fairy was beautiful, with bright blue eyes and golden hair, and cheeks like the damask rose; forever she would run out to the entrance of the cave, saying: "It will soon go down," meaning the water, and forever passing to and fro, up and down the cave, restless and always the first to pass out of the cave.

The third was quiet, but always busy, making everything in their home pleasant, and always doing something at the farther end of the cave.

Whenever the tide was out, the three fairies would pass from the cave and visit their mother in her beautiful home above. What was said and heard there I will one day tell, but the first named fairy would return with calmer face and brighter eyes than before. The second would be even more lovely and joyous, and the third more thoughtful and busy. One day after they had visited their mother, these three beautiful sisters sat near the entrance to their home, watching the in-coming tide. The first one did not speak; the second one said: "We will not always live here; I wonder why we cannot stay with our mother in her beautiful world?" The first one said: "It will not be long, we can wait." The third one hurried to

the farther end of the cave and was busy with
her loving duties.

One day when the first and second faries
were visiting their mother, they observed their
sister was not there and much wondered.   On
returning to their home in the cave they found
her not, but at the farther end of the cave a light
shone, and following it they saw a passage way
leading away, away into brightness; on and on
they went until they found themselves in their
mother's home and their sister was there; SHE
had made that pathway OUT of the cave to
the mother's home, and they no longer wait for
the ebbing of the tide, but can now pass to
and fro at will.

Who are the three fairies?   Who is their
mother?   What is the cave and the sea?

The *cave* in which the three fairies lived, is *human life*; the sea is outward circumstances, the
ebbing and flowing of the tide is life's changes.
The first fairy is *Faith*, who waits with
perfect trust and patience, knowing her hour
will come.   The second fairy is *Hope*, who,
forever restless and joyous, flies on before.
The third fairy is *Good Works*, inspired by
Faith, encouraged by *Hope*, but without whom
both Hope and Faith were valueless.

The mother of these three beautiful sisters
is *Love*, whose home is in heaven, but between
whom and the cave of life below, Faith, Hope.
and Good Works forever have communion-

Faith can wait for circumstances to change, bringing her nearer to Love; Hope can forever brighten the way, but Good Works overcomes all circumstances and carves a passage to Love's home, so that every hour the mother of these three blessed fairies is near. Now you can see what is meant by a fairy tale.

JOE, THE HUNCHBACK.

[A Story Founded on Fact.]

CHAPTER I.

"PLEASE sir, can my little sister come in and get warm?"

This was said to Mr. Armstead, whose benign countenance had invited the petition. The smiling face of Mr. Armstead was lighted with a still finer glow when he turned and saw the little deformed figure, the black face and wonderful eyes of Joe, the hunchback.

"Certainly Joe, come in." The warm fire burned brightly in the huge base burner, and Mr. Armstead was still busy over his counter, but he glanced up to see that Joe's little sister was almost a baby, and had a bright oval face

and sparkling eyes, and was certainly not dark-
er than a quadroon. They stood warming
themselves and looking at all the glass-ware
and chandeliers and other bright and beautiful
things in the place; presently a piano somewhere in the building struck up a tune. Joe's
sister, little Nell, listened in mute astonish-
ment and delight. "Has you dot a piany?"
she finally asked, walking up to Mr. Armstead
and listening all the time.

"Yes, I have one." Still little Nell listened
and then after several minutes asked: "Tan I
see the piany, Mr. Armstead?" "Well, I don't
know, perhaps." There was a merry twinkle
in his eye, and Joe thought he was quizzing, so
he said "yes Nell, see there," and he pointed
to a gas meter under the corner of the desk.

Joe was bright and knew when any one was
joking, so he said: "Thank ye sir," and took
Nells hand trudging out of the shop, and thinking Mr. Armstead was a splendid man, but
"very funny." Mr. Armstead called him back
and said, as he flipped him a quarter, "Joe,
please bring me some more kindlings, I like
those you brought before."

"Thankye sir, I will bring them to-day."
Joe and Nell passed out into the street, and
very gently and tenderly did he help her along.
A gentleman passing said: "How are you,
midget?" "How are you grasshopper?" said Joe,
and the tall gentleman smiled, thinking how

ready was the wit veiled in that little form, and wondering what the world had in store for "poor Joe" Some boys shouted after him "Joe, the hunchback, there goes Joe, the hunchback;" and Joe's eyes flashed, but he kept hold of little Nell's hand and said, "come on sis," while at first a look of defiance and then of pain crossed his pinched face, but his eyes, O, how they shone! They soon met a kind old lady, who spoke pleasantly, "Good morning children; Joe I see you are very good to your little sister, God will reward you."

"Don't want him to, Missus, don't want any reward for doin' what I likes to do, gits my pay right along." But he *thought*, "I would like to thrash them proud fellars that called me hunchback, 'spects I'll want some reward if I forgive them."

Pretty soon they were at home, a neat little white-washed house with just two rooms, and a little garden with radishes and onions and potatoes and corn. "Mammy" met them at the door, and said: "Dems good children, to come right back; did you do all the messages Joe?"

"Yes mammy, but—" "But what Joe, has somebody been cross, or dem bad boys been doin' tricks?"

Joe's face told that something had hurt him, but mammy only said, "De Lord says forgive dem dat injure you," and Joe thought of his kindling wood for Mr. Armstead and gave his "mammy" the quarter and ran off to get the wood.

--

CHAPTER II.

LITTLE Bessie Armstead was playing in the yard near her father's dwelling, there was a cistern near the corner of the garden, the water that was conveyed into the cistern from the roof of the house was used for watering the vegetables and plants. Some one had left the cistern open and just as Joe was entering the gate to announce that he had brought the load of kindlings, he heard a child scream and saw little Bessie disappear into the cistern. Mrs. Armstead, pale and terrified, came to the door just in time to see her darling fall from sight. It was the work of an instant, Joe caught a a strong rope, tied one end to the fence, made it secure, and without a moments hesitation threw of his coat and went down on the rope. holding on with one hand he felt for the little girl, caught her by the dress as she was sinking the second time and held her out of the water. Mrs. Armstead called for aid and some men working in an adjoining yard came, not a mo-

ment too soon, for Joe could not have held on
to the rope with one hand much longer. They
carefully aided him and his precious burden to
rise, making a noose of the ropes they brought,
and Joe was drawn up with the little girl, who
was unconscious but was soon restored. Joe
was not very strong and the shock prostrated
him for weeks, but he was tenderly cared for
by "mammy" who had now a double burden,
since Joe's little earnings helped to "keep the
wolf from the door."

Mr. and Mrs. Armstead, with hearts over-
flowing with gratitude to Joe for saving their
precious Bessie, were untiring in their atten-
tions, and many little delicacies found their
way to the bedside of poor Joe, and he too,
had other compensations. Mr. Armstead drop-
ped in one day and noticed Joe's eyes fixed on
some far away vision, he sat down softly on a
chair by the bedside and heard Joe whisper:

"Dat's Massa Jesus, 1 see him shine, Oh! and
dar is little sister Lily, white as snow, no black
faces dar." Mr. Armstead thought Joe was
going to die and believed this was the warn-
ing, but Joe soon turned over smiling and said:

"Good morning Mr. Armstead I feel better
and shall soon be well." Then he told him in
very graphic language what he had seen, and
that the "Good Jesus" had told him to get well
again, but that he could never be straight and
tall, like other boys. "The master said that

is your cross Joe,' and I 'spose I mus' bear it."

Mr. Armstead was in deep meditation that day when he went home to his noon-day meal.

"Wife I begin to think the days of miracles and visions are not over yet," he said after a long silence.

"I never have thought they were, I believe we have spirits all about us," she said.

"Yes, I know you always said so but that little Joe has convinced me." Then he related what Joe had seen and said, and Mrs. Armstead listened with tears in her eyes, saying after a pause:

"I believe some guardian angel helped Joe to save our Bessie, he looked like an angel that day."

—

CHAPTER III.

JOE was on his feet again and could do his part toward helping "mammy"— running of errands, cutting and selling kindlings, and doing odd jobs about the village. But the far away look in his eyes, and their unwonted lustre still remained.

"Mammy" had a kind of awe of Joe. She undertook to teach, and sometimes scold him, but the words would die on her lips, and she would be half frightened with herself thinking aloud. "De Lord tells dat chile ebery thing—dars no use in trying to teach him!"

One day Joe went to do some "chores" and little things for Mrs. Blake, wife of Lawyer Blake. They were well to do people, and the villagers had great respect for the legal lore of "Simeon Blake, Attorney and Counsellor at Law." But Mr. Blake was an "Infidel" to orthodox Christianity, and it grieved his little wife sorely, and annoyed his neighbors because he would not identify himself with any house of worship.

When he came home to tea the evening of the day Joe was there, he said to Mrs. Blake: "I see you have Hunchback Joe here. What a strange mixture of shrewdness and superstition he is, to be sure." He had not looked at his wife, but when he did, he saw her usually calm face very pale and agitated, and she seemed to have been waiting to tell him something.

"What is the matter my dear; are you ill?" "No, but if it had not been for Joe the house would have been robbed of everything valuable."

"How was it wife? I guess you was a little nervous!" "No wait until you hear," said Mrs. Blake. "You know that the painters had been using the long ladder, and left it against the house. I had been very busy all day in the

back part of the house; and Joe was pulling
weeds and attending to something in the garden. At noon the painters went away, and
just then I heard something fall, and I sort of
screamed. When I ran to the side door, there
was Joe pulling down the ladder."

"Misses Blake, lock all the doors, there's a
thief in there." "I had locked the door of my
room when I came down. And now a tramp
had gone up the ladder, and Joe had pulled the
ladder down and the man was in our room.
Had you not been out of town Joe would have
gone for you, but as it was, he kept watch and
we hailed the first neighbor that went by, who
happened to be parson Brownlow. He was very
much excited, and wanted a revolver to go up
to the room. I reminded him that an officer
of the law would be better, and he ran to the
police station. The poor wretch above, seeing
he was cut off from retreat by the ladder, evidently tried all the doors and the windows, and
finally in sheer desperation, scrambled out over
the porch and let himself fall to the ground on
the other side of the house, and before the
parson and policeman returned, he was gone.
But he stole nothing, and I think he was pursued, but I havn't heard whether he was caught;
and Joe he stood all the time watching me and
telling me "not to be feared," for no harm could
come. I feel grateful to Joe, for had I been
alone there might have been something worse."

Mr. Blake was quite pale, and said aloud, "Joe is brave and we must do all we can for him, but you, my dear are quite used up with this affair, so please think no more of it; we'll thank our stars that nothing worse came of it."

But this was not the end.

—

CHAPTER IV.

THE officers of the law were after the thieves who attempted in so bold and daring a manner to enter Mr. Blake's house and rob it in daylight. But Joe did not relish that part of the business, somehow he wished they had a "fair chance" to know about "Massa Jesus," he believed they would do better. Valiant as he had been in protecting Mrs. Blake and in saving Bessie Armstead from drowning, he shrank from hunting those outlaws who it seemed to him, were more to be pitied than blamed. Joe's was a small body and a small brain for reasoning, men thought, but his brain was light and his eyes bright, and there was a kind of feeling that seemed like a sixth sense, he knew things beforehand; so when he went home that night he was not surprised to find a

young girl about thirteen years old sitting
quite close to mammy, with a hunted look upon her face, that changed into a smile as she
saw Joe, and became very pretty when she saw
there was no danger. She had a guitar and
when the curtains were drawn she sang soft
and low some sweet songs to Joe and mammy
and little Nell, the latter soon falling asleep in
mammy's arms.

Lita, for that was the young girl's name, had
been seen by Joe hovering around lawyer
Blake's house before and at the time when the
thieves were there; she won him by her pale,
hunted look and he whispered to her:

"You'd better go Miss to where it's safe, for
I've seen the man go up to that window by the
ladder, he'll be catched sure, and you don't
look like a thief Miss."

So he showed her in an instant the way to
mammy's house, and she needed the care and
rest that she found there. But every time the
door would open or a noise was heard outside,
she would start and grow pale.

"Don't be scared chile," said mammy, "if
ye's innercent as yer looks no harm can come
for its the lambs He cares for."

Mammy did'nt press Lita to tell her story,
she took her in because Joe had sent her, and
after Joe had told mammy all he knew about
Lita, still the girl was not questioned nor sus-

pected. Lita sang the following little song
with music on the guitar:

" 'Twas a little bird and a nest,
So sweet, so sweet,
All day long could birdie rest,
Ti wheet, ti wheet
All day, all day.

" Why did the little bird fly away?
Ah me, ah me,
From the nest afar to stray,
Sad is she, sad is she,
All day, all day.

And the tears would roll down mammy's
cheeks when she thought perhaps Lita was the
" little bird."

CHAPTER V.

THEY were enjoying themselves in the
little home of " mammy," when Joe's
quick ear caught the sound of several footsteps, and Lita again started
as if fearing some danger. Joe was
about to motion Lita to some place
of concealment, but he was too late,
and presently a rap on the door was followed
by the entrance of the sheriff and two consta-

bles and a man with shrewd eyes and sinister expression, who said:

That is the girl, sir, I tracked her here." And sure enough they had come to arrest Lita; mammy protested in vain that she believed her "more sinned against than sinning." And Joe with a strange light in his eyes, said softly to her as he slid closely to her side, "De angels will keep you Miss, never fear." So, as they would not permit Joe to accompany her to the jail, where the matron really received the girl quite kindly, and even the brusque jailor looked pityingly upon her. She was examined and some portion of goods stolen from an adjoining town two or three days previous, proved sufficient cause for her detention, although she could give but little information concerning the perpetrators of the theft; she seemed shocked and stunned, and afraid of the sinister looking man who had accompanied the officers to "Mammy's" house and pointed her out to them. From him she visibly shrank like a flower, and the officer in charge noticed the evil look the man (nominally a detective) had, so he resolved to stand between the young girl and any greater evil than that which had come to her to-night.

Joe could not rest, so hurried over toward lawyer Blake's house, and seeing a light ventured to go to the door of his study, which was on the ground floor and entered from the porch;

he rapped and Mr. Blake came to the French window which also served for a door. "What Joe, you here! I hope nothing is wrong with Mammy or little Nell!"

Joe told him briefly and very distinctly all knew about Lita, and said: "I know you is a lawyer sir, and I thought you had a kind heart, and if you'll jes look into court when they brings her out to-morrow ye'll see she's not done any wrong."

Mr. Blake carefully noted down all Joe told him, and assured him he would certainly interest himself in the case. Then Joe walked around by the jail but seeing no way to communicate with any one, he was compelled to go home and wait till morning.

When Joe told Mammy what he had done, she said: "Well, Massa Blake does not fear God but he loves his children and that is just as good, if not better."

Joe dreamed that night of rescuing Lita from the sinister looking detective and taking her away to a place of safety where Jesus and the angels were, and how happy he felt when the Master said: "Joe you have a soul white as snow," and he awoke hearing heavenly music, and one voice sounded like Lita's.

CHAPTER VI.

JOE could hardly "possess his soul in patience" until the morning; then he hurried away to Lawyer Blake's as early as he thought would be proper, but not seeing any token in the study of Mr. Blake's presence he walked around the house, Mrs. Blake saw him and beckoned him to come into the dining room, where they sat talking, having just finished breakfast.

"Now tell us Joe, all you know about that girl yonder," said Mr. Blake. Joe knew he meant Lita, so he told him about seeing her hanging around the day the thief entered Mrs. Blake's room, that he saw she looked so "misable like" that he thought she didn't belong to the thief, and he told her to go to "mammy's" for he felt sure the thief would be caught then he thought she would have to go to jail. "But yer see Mister Blake. I don't think she *is* a thief."

"You confess do you not, that appearances are against her," said the lawyer. "Yes I know," Joe said, as the strange bright look came into his eyes, "but Mister Blake, I has my reasons, sometimes *I'm told* things."

"Who tells you Joe, and what things do you

mean?" said the man of learning, well knowing about Joe's strange sayings. "Well I don't
know as you'll understand, Mister Blake, but I
have another voice to talk to me sometimes, and
the angels say she is one of 'God's little ones
who must not be harmed.'" He turned to Mrs.
Blake, whose eyes were full of tears as she
murmured, "She is so young too, there must
be some great wrong somewhere." Joe low-
ered his voice and said half hesitatingly yet
still fearlessly, "Mr. Blake, who is that 'detective,' does he belong here in this town?" "No
Joe I think not, at least I never saw him; perhaps the sheriff knows him; I see you have
your doubts of him; it takes a rogue to catch a
rogue they say, and maybe this 'detective'
knows more about the robberies than this poor
girl." Then turning to Joe he said, "Come to
me at ten at the court room." Joe left the
pleasant room, and in it were two warm hearts
interested in the fate of poor Lita.

"Do you know dear," said Lawyer Blake,
"Joe is a riddle to me, sometimes I think he
will convert me to a belief in the supernatural."
Mrs. Blake smiled sweetly yet was silent, too
discreet to break the spell that had evidently
been woven around her husband's mind, but
inwardly praying, "God grant it may be so."

Joe went home to see if Mammy and Nell
wanted anything, he attended to all the errands
and took another load of wood to Mr. Arm-

stead's; as he was returning he met Mr. Armstead looking more agitated than was his wont,
but he stopped to speak to Joe and say, "Joe
I've been robbed of fifty dollars; not much it is
true, but more than a poor man can afford to
loose.   I saw the rascal just as he left the shop
and tried to follow him but he evaded me; I'm
going down to the court house to look for the
sheriff, all the constables are there on account
of that pretty they arrested with stolen goods."

CHAPTER VII.

THE court room was crowded, whether
the fame of Lita's youth and beauty
had been noised abroad, or whether
the floating population of the town had
nothing better to do than to attend
the court, one could hardly guess.

The court opened with one or two
cases of petty larceny and then the young girl
Lita was brought before the court.

She was deadly pale and her eyes wore the
same hunted, frightened look, only more in-
tense than before.   It was evident that she wa
very weak, either from physical exhaustion or
from fear, or mental agony of some sort.

The Judge gave a start when he looked at

her, and seemed unwilling to address one so young, as charged with crime, or complicity in crime.

"Will the prisoner stand?" Lita was unable to do so and the chair at first placed in the dock to receive her, still held her almost fainting form. What is your name? Her lips moved but no articulate sound came from them; one of the attorneys leaned forward and caught the whispered "Lita, sir." A murmur of sympathy ran through the court room, and "mammy" who was present, sobbed aloud.

"Lita, and what other name?" No answer came, and the court proceeded to read the charge against the prisoner. She was accused of complicity in the theft, stolen property having been found upon her person, and she having been seen in company with a person known to have robbed several houses on the night before Mr. Blake's house was entered; she was seen near Mr. Blake's, and was traced to the house of Joe, the hunchback, who seemed to know her.

Joe was called, Lita seemed somewhat relieved by his presence. The prosecuting attorney, after whispering with the "detective" before mentioned in this narrative, said: "What is your name?" "Joe Williams." "Occupation?" "Odd jobs sir, sells kindlings, works in gardens and about houses sir," "Have you no regular occupation?" "No-sir, the likes of me can't

very well learn a trade, but I do work hard all
the same sir." Joe was well known in the town
and many an approving nod was seen in the
crowd.

"Do you know the prisoner, Joe?" "I know
her a little sir; I'd like to tell jes what I know."
"No, answer the questions I ask please. Now
Joe tell us how and where you first came to
know the prisoner?,,

"Saw her on the street sir, in front of Mr.
Blakes house, thought she looked lonesome
and hungry and I told her to run to mammy's"
"Had you not seen her before?" "No sir."
'Was she with any one?' 'No, sir.' 'Did you
know what she had on her person, I mean the
watch and other things, since found to be stol-
en goods?' 'No, sir.' 'Did you see her speak
with any one?' 'Yes, sir, I saw her speak to
the man who went up the ladder into Mr.
Blakes' house.' 'Did she seem to know him?'
Don't know, sir, she might have asked for
alms." Did she tell you anything about herself or her history?"

Counsel objected.

Mr. Blake, who had in answer to the question put to Lita whether she had legal counsel,
volunteered his services, now objected to that
question; it could not be evidence, he said, and
was sustained by the court.

Examination resumed.

"Did you see her speak to the man after he

came out of Mr. Blake's house?" "No, sir, she was gone and he ran away." "Why did you send her to your own house?" "Cause I thought she might be one of Jesus' little lambs out in the cold."

"That will do."

Joe's direct and straight-forward answers carried conviction to every mind that he spoke truly.

The evidence was taken of the stolen goods being found on Lita, of the fact that she had been seen before entering the town, in company with a notorious character, who was supposed to be the thief.

Just then Mr. Armstead entered, glanced around the room and disappeared. Joe's mammy saw him; Mr. Blake saw him.

The testimony of the "detective was about being taken, when Lita, seeing who it was, gave a shriek and fell into a swoon. She was taken away, and Mr. Armstead entered, saying to a sheriff "Arrest your man." The sheriff took the detective by the arm and said: "I arrest this man on charge of theft." Mr. Armstead said a few words to Mr. Blake, Mr. B. spoke to the Judge and the latter said:

"The court cannot proceed to-day; the young girl Lita is discharged as a prisoner, no charge having been sustained against her, but she is detained as a witness; Mr. Blake, I trust her

to your charge in consideration of the pledge
you have given that she shall appear when summoned."

CHAPTER VIII.

A STRANGE feeling had crept into
the heart of Judge Warren, the magistrate before whom the young girl
Lita had been brought as a prisoner
that day; an unaccountable tenderness. His life had been a lonely one
and filled with a sad and almost trag-
ic interest. Only a few of his personal friends
knew the particulars of his domestic sorrow, and
these kindly forebore any reference to a past
that must be painful in the extreme to one who
always seemed so silent and so far away in his
thoughts. A busy life in his legal profession,
and now in the capacity of magistrate, had
served to keep him from brooding over his
lonely life. As he walked home his thoughts
were busy with the past, with the dead joys
and blighted hopes that once were full of
brightness. He muttered something to himself that a passer by heard, "Am I mad that
this wild fancy has taken possession of me?"

The passer by looked up in surprise to hear so strange an utterance from Judge Warren, but seeing his abstracted mood, passed on without a word.

That night Lita stayed in the bright and cheerful home of Lawyer Blake, and never did mother more tenderly care for her own than this good Christian woman (in the true Christ spirit, for Mrs. Blake was no hypocrite) care for this child ; she was weak and unstrung from the scene in the court room, but Lita needed her every care : long time did she lie in a deep swoon, pale as death and like a marble statue. She might have been carved for a face and figure of misery had it not been so very youthful, so full of something that *would* appeal to brighter things.

Lita remained in the little room adjoining Mrs. Blake's, fitted up for a her as a bedroom, that she might receive every attention, and there, flitting in and out, Mrs. Blake attended to the wants, and prayed over this waif "who might be one of His little ones." During the evening Judge Warren entered Mr. Blake's study or library with a singular feeling and beating of the heart as he asked for the welfare of the young girl, and desired Mr. Blake to tell him all he knew about her.

Mr. Blake narrated what Joe had told him about seeing Lita with the man who entered his (Mr. Blake's) house, that Joe thought she

looked homesick, and sent her to " mammy's,"
and that nothing more was known, only, said
Mr. Blake, we all see that she is more 'sinned
against than sinning ;' it is written on every
feature."

"Is that all you know, Mr. Blake?" asked
Judge Warren, in a very earnest voice.   " Pos-
itively all, but I will try to find out more from
that rascally detective, for Mr. Armstead has
engaged me to try him, and of course it will
be in your court, Judge, and / believe he is
somehow mixed up in this whole affair ; I am
sure he is no detective of the right sort, and
Armstead can swear he is the man who robbed his money drawer of $50.00 in broad day-
light."

Judge Warren soon took his leave, only
wondering still at his strange interest in the
young outcast girl.

CHAPTER IX.

JOE had a strange dream or vision the night after the events related in the last chapter. He saw a beautiful lady, an angel, it seemed to him, who came close to his humble bed and touching him with her cool, soft hand, said : "I thank you from my heavenly home for restoring my child to her father's arms ; I am the mother of Lita ; I died of sorrow when she was stolen from us."

Joe awoke with her ' God bless you ' ringing in his ears ; he remembered every word, he saw how the angel lady resembled Lita, and wondered who the father of Lita could be. He called mammy, for he could not sleep, and told her every word and all he had seen in the vision. "Now mammy, what shall I do?" said Joe.

" Wait chile, de Lord leads you in his own way," said mammy fervently. Joe remained in prayer until the dawn of day, then having taken a little breakfast, but too full of his vision to eat much, he hastened to the house of Mr. Blake (*he* was a true friend and would hear him and know what to do), so mused Joe as he

went along, being led by the angel lady, though
then he did not see her.

"What! is that you Joe, at this early hour?"
said Mr. Blake, who had stepped out on the
verandah for a breath of fresh air.

"Yes, sir, can I see you in yer—study sir?"
said Joe, hesitating over the word 'study,' as
he had sometimes heard the library called.

"Certainly my boy, come in," and Joe followed Mr. Blake in and closed the door.—
"Now, what is it?" for Mr. Blake read, as he
had learned to do, the bright lustre in Joe's
eyes, and he knew he had something of im-
portance to communicate.

Joe said: "I've had more visions sir, and
they have told me things." Then Joe told his
'dream' of the previous night with such accu-
racy that Mr. Blake knew he had seen and
heard (or believed he had) all that he told.

Mr. Blake grew pale as Joe went on, for after
the visit of Judge Warren the evening before,
he too, had been busy with the past in sympathy with his friend, but he only said: "What
you have told me is very strange Joe, say
nothing about it; but I have learned to know
that your dreams always mean something."

Just as Joe was leaving, Mr. Armstead came
in and said hurriedly, "Mr. Blake, come down
to the jail, the keeper says that fellow is dying
and he wants to see you or Judge Warren."
Mr. Blake went for the Judge and hastened

with Mr. Armstead to the poor wretch who had evidently taken poison; too late now to render him aid. The physician in charge of prisoners had asked for other aid, the priest was there, Judge Warren was there almost as soon as they. The prisoner motioned to the Judge and said in a low but clear voice:

"I'm dying Judge Warren, and these are my last words, as God hears me they are true; Lita is your child, stolen from the very door of your dwelling in revenge for a trifling punishment which I received through you at the hands of justice; my name is Dan Drake, and I have been a wanderer and a criminal always, but no harm has come to her, for I meant to send her back as soon as the reward was large enough; Billy Reves is my pal, but he'd have harmed the girl if I had not made him fear I'd hand him over to you judge. I wanted money, but that's all over now. I saw the girl's mother last night just as she looked and screamed when she saw me grab up the little un and tote her off, but she didn't look angry, only smiled, with a sorry look in her eyes; yer can't pray for me Judge—but—don't—curse"

Here the poor fellow gasped for breath, a higher tribunal had received the spirit of the sham detective. The Judge gave orders for a funeral, asked the jailor to see everything prepared for the funeral on the day after the morrow. and then with pale, yet joyous face, with more elasticity than his step had known for years, he walked to the house of his friend , Joe was there.   Mr. Blake took his wife aside and in a few moments Judge Warren was in the presence of his daughter, named for her dead mother Lititia; they called her Lita.   And never was there greater joy than in the hearts of father and daughter.   Mr. and Mrs. Blake in tears ; Mr. and Mrs. Armstead rejoicing— the whole town full of thanksgiving for the restoration of the little girl lost so long ago and restored to her father's arms.

"Joe, you've converted me," said Mr. Blake, and Joe, looking up with the lustre in his eyes, said. "No, sir ; the good Lord has done it ; the angel lady is glad ; I'm going home.

He went home to mammy's, and that night the angels bore him to their home.   He had done his work, and he told mammy he would be near to bless her.

The whole town turned out to the funeral, and next to mammy and little Nell, Judge and Lita, Mr. and Mrs. Armstead and Bessie, and Mr. and Mrs. Blake, were those nearest the casket.

SPRING

[A Drama, enacted every year.]

ACT I.

EARTH (speaks.)

I FEEL the ancient splendor of the Sun draw me across equinoxial bars into the solstice of the Spring. Again I feel the icy fetters melt and fade, and tremblings of dear delight that pierce with joy my timeworn, aged breast anew. I seem to wake as from a long, long sleep, and in that slumber all my form was clothed in snowy vestments, like the sleep called death. Ice-fetters bound me, and my prisoned powers could give no answer to the calling stars, or to the waves of ether throbbing 'round. What do I hear? A voice in golden sounds seems to allure me on to life again! Once more my spirit leaps to greet the Sun.

SUN (speaks).

Waken thou slumbering earth! Long time with kisses
    warm
I've touched thy brow and cheek, I've breathed upon thy
    form:
Long time my rays have pressed the northern winter king
Back to his northern quest; long time the waiting Spring
Has leaned over my car, listening for thee to wake.
Sending thee from afar sweet breathings for my sake.

O, Earth, thou child of mine, through space and matter
    blent.
In me thy beauties shine, to thee my warm rays sent.
Revive the powers of old and thou art young again;

Splendors and wealth untold of beauty thou'l retain.

SPRING (speaks.)

Waken, waken! O, Earth, I am the spirit of all birth!
I come in the rays of the Sun, toward me all life must run.
Rootlets and germs, all hidden, I breathe upon unbidden:
They hear me, and their feet hasten all voices silent--
    sweet:

All birds and living things make answer with their wings
And with their breath of song, to me their chimes belong.
I touch thee, till the too, I pierce thy brown hills through
With emerald spears of grass, with throbbings as I pass.

I am a spirit aflame: all forms are mine, each name,
Every flower and leaf, every breath of the life that con-
    quers death.
Waken thou, O, Earth! unto me the Sun from his throne
    calls thee.
I am his messenger, Summer's blest harbinger.

WINTER, (departing, but growling angrily), speaks to the
    sun and earth.

"Go, must I? Ha, ha, ha, ho: hear the chains rattle, the
    trumpets blow.
I am the King of ice and snow, but you say I must "go,"
    "go," "go."
I held my power over the Earth, she was my slave: there
    was my dearth.
Death and I held our reign of mirth, with us there never
    can be birth.

I go, but my chief will remain, the north wind he will
    cause you pain.
Each early flower he will regain, ha, ha: I slowly yield
    my reign
Tender buds and blossoms rare, he will steal on them un-
    aware,
Many HUMAN blossoms fair, he will wither, for he dare.

But when we have them they are dust, all we gain is
  mould and rust!
Baffled are we? God is just, Spirit lives as live it must.
I go, I go, but I'll come once more, when Spring and
  Summer bloomings are oe'r.
When Autumn all its wealth doth pour, I'll take the
husks just as before.

––––

ACT II.

FLORA (speaks.)

COME my children, ye bright flowers, come
I call ye with my voice of tender love;
Arbutus, answer from your silent home;
Hepaticas spring beauties—nearer me move!

Starry Anemone wake robin! all,
Come ye wild Hyacinths Violets, come!
Ye hear my voice, ye answer to my call:
The warm winds woo ye and the wild bees hum.

Ye ferns and mosses in the dewy dell,
Unfold ye trees, ye birchen tassels fair,
Ye maple buds, ye chestnut blossoms swell,
Unfurl your banners in the spring time air.

Nay, fear not, tho' the north wind blows awhile,
He shall not touch you, precious ones' ne'r fear:
Do you not feel your mother's tender smile?
Darlings co me forth, for love and spring are here.

ARBUTUS (speaks.)

Mother Flora, I hear your loved voice,
And it bids my heart rejoice! rejoice!
Now the icy fetters are broken,
Now the words of love are spoken.

I bring my rose-tinted offering,
Mine the first flowers of spring,
Waxen and fragrant 'mid the brown leaves,
Like hopes arisen in a heart that grieves.

I am the symbol of early love,
Near me all sweet hopes must move,
O, mother Flora, I come again,
To prove that winter cannot remain.

ROBIN (sings.)

  te-whit, te-whit, te-whit,
The north wind don't frighten me a bit.
We can build our nest on the sunny side
Of the cottage there where young lovers bide;
They are mated love, and so are we,
My mate and I, happy as we can be.

  The-trol, the-trol, tra la sweet,
How many friends we already meet;
Dear husband how do my feathers look?
Your's are as bright as a nice new book.
The married pair are glad we've come
To build our nest in the porch of their home.

  Ah sweet' ah sweet, ah sweet,
Make haste, be swift with wings and feet,
For spring is here, we must build our nest
And be very loving—this *lace* is best,
I saw the bride put it on the grass,
It must be for us—she saw us pass.
  Ah sweet, ah sweet.

ACT III.

VIOLETS (speak.)

WE come, we come, in the woody glen.
Where the mossy bank is found;
In the meadow bright, on field and fen
We scatter the sky around.

For our eyes are blue— as we came through
From the home of light above,
As we came by the tint of the sky
Was into our petals wove.

We come to cheer the heart that is sad.
To bloom before loving eyes,
To make little children humble and glad
We bring messages from the skies:

For *your* eyes are blue —as *you* came through
From the home of light above.
You borrowed the ray, the *blue* of the day,
To beam in your eyes of love.

BUTTERCUP (speaks.)

Buttercups, buttercups, starry and bright.
Here we are with our goblets of light.
On the meadow, beside the stream,
Everywhere, everywhere, just like a dream.

Sunshine is woven into our hearts.
Every bright petal rich gladness imparts;
Baby eyes glisten whene'r they behold
Our yellow blossoms, brighter than gold.

We are like sunbeams nor stately nor tall,

But we can shine in the spring   in the fall,
Doing our share to brighten the earth,
Glad of our brightness, glad of our birth.

THE GRASSES (speak.)

Here are a million spears of green,
Piercing the darkness, where winter has been;
Now we can spread the carpet for your feet,
Making a frame-work for the flowers sweet.

We are not warriors fighting for renown,
Our jeweled swords but win a dewy crown,
We are the "body guard" of Flora and her train,
Making a pathway for sunshine and rain.

By the hedge, near the stream, in the meadow and
   field,
Where e'er there is room, we *our* blade can yield;
So if one deed of beauty finds room here to grow,
Like grass it will spread o'er the whole earth below.

WIND-FLOWER* (speaks.)

Here are my blossoms starry and bright
   Palest of rose color tinted with blue,
With the warm wind I come into sight,
   Tinted and varied with many a hue.

First without leaves, only blossoms appear,
   Hastening ever to greet the young spring;
Crowning with beauty the joyous new year,
   Nodding and smiling at everything.

Then I must die, and up from the roots
   New stem and leaf make a delicate stalk,
And out of this my new blossom shoots,
   Pale as a star bloom in heaven's walk.

Even as spirit *in* body am I,
   When I first blossom to beauty and light;

*Hepatica — Anemone.

As soul disembodied in the sky,
  Is my next blooming, as pure and as bright.

RAIN (speaks.)

Sprinkle, drop, drop, patter, patter,
  Here we come in joy again,
Out of clouds flying and flying,
  Gladsome, gleeful spring-time rain.

Little crystal balls of laughter,
  Chasing all the boys and girls
Through the fields and we run after,
  Resting on their cheeks and curls.

Kissing all the buds and blossoms,
  All the trees and blades of grass,
Resting in the wind-flower's bosom,
  Gaily sparkling as you pass.

Murmur, murmur, twinkle, murmur,
  Now we flood the fields again;
Such rare planting time and sowing,
  Cometh after spring's warm rain.

ACT IV.

EARTH (sings.)

NOW all my pulses thrill anew
  With life and wondrous love
Now every floweret gemmed with dew,
  Comes forth my joy to prove.

Now *Phœbus*(1) mounts his chariot
  Each day for my delight.
By no divinity forgot
  New pleasures greet my sight.

Flora(2) comes forth with all her train,
   Collona(3) crowns the hills.
Orpheus(4) sings his glad refrain,
   Sweet *Pan*(5) his piping trills.

Diana(6) sends her silvery boat,
   Laden with purest flowers,
'Mong *Naiades*(7) and Nymphs(8) below,
   To deck the Fairie's(9) bowers.

The mated birds sing in the groves,
   The doves and swallows come,
Eros(10) revives the eden(11) loves
   And finds his primal home.

FLORA, THE FLOWERS. LEAVES, GRASSES, BIRDS. RAIN.
STREAMS, CHILDREN AND ALL LIVING THINGS (sing.)

Joy! Joy! the Spring is here again,
   The earth is beautiful and glad,
Waking from the long winter pain,
   No longer cold, silent and sad.

Rejoice! Rejoice! all things that live,
   For *being* O, sing and rejoice!
Your praises to the Giver give,
   In sweetest and most solemn voice.

FLORA AND THE FLOWERS GRASSES AND LEAVES (sing.)

We praise, we praise the *Giver good*,
   For life, for beauty's wondrous dower.
We praise him in the solitude,
   We praise him in each glen and bower.

1, Phœbus, the God of day, the sun; 2, Flora, the Goddess (mother) of the flowers; 3, Collona, the Goddess of the hills; 4, Orpheus, the God of the winds, 5, Pan, the God of music, the inventor of the first musical instrument formed of reeds; 6, Diana, the moon, the Goddess of the woods and of purity; 7, 8, 9, Naiades, Nymphs and Faries; spirits of the waters, woods and fountains; 10, Eros, the God of love: 11, state of happiness and beauty.

We praise him on the hill and plain,
  We praise him in the garden fair,
We praise him in a sweet refrain.
  We *bloom* in praises *everywhere*.

BIRDS (sing.)

We sing and praise, we sing and praise
  From dawn of day to set of sun.
We fly and chirp, and sing our praise.
  Until our life of joy is done.

We praise him when upon the wing.
  We praise him in our nest so fair,
We praise him when our songs we sing.
  We *sing* and praise him everywhere.

RAIN, STREAMS AND FOUNTAINS (sing.)

We praise the "Giver of all good,"
  In crystal waters bright and clear,
We murmur in the distant wood,
  We sparkle in the streamlet near.

We patter, murmur, flow our praise.
  We water germs of flowers fair,
Silent, in many *voiceless* ways,
  We *flow* in praises every where.

CHILDREN, LARGE AND SMALL, (sing.)

We praise thee Father, Mother, God,
  That life and love can conquer death,
We praise him for the verdant sod,
  We praise him for each pulse and breath.

For every beauty of the spring,
  For fields of grass and blooming flowers,
For song of birds, their matchless wing.
  The waters, all life giving powers.

For earth and air and sky above,
  For body and for raiment here.

But chiefly for the gift of love
That conquers death's dark winter fear.

For the *soul's spring-time*, O. parent soul.
We praise thee in our thoughts most rare.
In *deeds* inspired by loves control.
We love and praise thee every where.

CROWN OF LILIES.

Given to Mrs. Nettie P. Fox, by Ouina, through the lips of her medium, Water Lily (Mrs. C. L. V. Richmond), at the residence of Dr. and Mrs. Douglass, Ottumwa, Iowa, Tuesday evening, Aug. 29, 1882.

IF life's path were made of flowers.
    And life's flowers were made of gems.
And the treasures in life's bowers.
    Were the spirit's diadem;

If along the weary way.
    Sometimes around the faltering feet
You could see the brightness play.
    And linger around, and greet.

There never would be a time
    When the mornings were not aglow.
And the noon-day all sublime.
    And when music did not flow.

For within the heart enwound;
    Within the spirit and above.
There is no token there, nor sound.
    Prompted not by truth and love.

There is no uttered thought within
    That does not seek the height.
The highest height, free from din.
    And glamour of mortal night.

And there is no gift or grace
   Thou wouldst not to others give,
Even in thine appointed place
   To them, if *they* could live
Purer, wiser and more free,
   Because of the gift from thee.

And out of pain, sorrow, or care
   The golden shrine is set,
And the angels, to thee unaware,
   Place there life's amulet.

I crown thee now with its pure light,
   As the spirit is crowned from above,
I consecrate the soul to right
   The *Crown of Lilies* of Love.

SHIELD OF LIFE AND STANDARD OF TRUTH.

Given to Col. D. M. Fox by Ouina, through the lips of her medium "Water Lily" (Mrs. Cora L. V. Richmond), at the residence of Dr. & Mrs. Douglass, Ottumwa, Iowa, August 29, 1882.

THERE is no lukewarmness, whate'er
   Thou dost, thou dost with mind
And heart and soul and brain,
   Whatever else we *here* can find
No half way, the mind tracing one thing,
The heart another, from its secret spring

Opens its source and every power
   Subservient to this stream must flow:
There is no hidden dream, no dower
   By other paths, or straighter go,
No hidden purpose, but the will
To do and be, one thing to fill.

And that thing is the highest thought
  Thy brain can know thy heart can feel,
Whatever of life is outwrought,
  Whatever heaven may reveal.

So in the past when worshiping
  Beside another shrine,
Thy heart was there, the probing wing
  Of thy whole life made it divine—
When out of it thy spirit came,
So came its inward flame.

There is ready sympathy of heart,
  Ready tears for other's woe;
A hand such strength here to impart
  As in the mind may flow.

But chiefly life devoted still
  To the one purpose, truth on earth,
Its message here thus to fulfill,
  And consecrate its heavenly birth.

Strong are the powers that bend above,
  Bright are the angels 'round thy way,
The recompense of purest love,
  That from the fountain stream doth sway,
Oh! take thou this *Shield of Life*
  And *Standard of Truth*, free from strife.

"LIFE'S CRYSTAL STAR."

[Name Poem, Given by Ouina, to Mrs. Hull, Materializing Medium, at her home in Brooklyn, March 13, 1882.]

EVEN as a crystal drop of dew,
In which the stars of Heaven may shine,
Or as an atmosphere bright, through
Which glow images most divine:

Or as a gem, wherein the light
Reflects the beauties of the sky,
So thy spirit, hidden from sight,
Reveals that heaven and love are nigh.

As silent-bright as jewels set
Within the heart of mother earth,
By Faith placed in Love's Coronet,
Triumphant over outward birth:

As crystal as dew-drop of morn
That trembles in the lily's breast,
As radiant as a night in June
When stars climb up at Heaven's behest:

As faithful perfect in thy faith
And truth, even as the Polar Star,
These and thy love would conquer death,
And triumph where immortals are.

But when the light shall be revealed,
Wherein are traced thy deeds of love,
Sweet flowers that often lie concealed,
And images of heaven above,
Transfigured then, as one afar,
Shalt thou be placed.

"RUBY FLOWER."

[A Name Poem, by Ouina, given to little Carrie Miller Cook, of
Brooklyn, Grand-daughter of Chas. R. Miller, of the "Psychome-
tric Circular."]

FROM out the spirit bowers
Come the sweet children of earth,
Little buds and flowers
That bloom to heavenly birth.
And from the spirit home attend
Angels forever bright and fair,
When they unto the earth descend,
Ever these flowrets rare:
They flutter round your way,
Like birds in summer time,
Warbling sweet songs alway
And give a gladsome chime.

A special gift was sent
When this sweet child was given,
Tokens of love-light lent,
A jewel bright from heaven.
And ministering ones
Attend her earthly way,
Guiding her tender feet
Lest thorns shall near them stay;
And gifts like crystal stars,
Hang 'round and o'er her brow,
As softest breath of summer
Morning moves the bough.

Love bends around her way
Like rainbows over head,
And forms of little ones

In heaven above her tread,
Moving ever to and fro,
Giving tokens of their love.
Each added year shall give
Added light and power to prove
That beings from above
Pass ever near your sight,
Anew unfold their love,
Like blossoms in sun-light.

O, as roses are the words
Of childhood folded here,
As gladsome as young birds,
As full of loving cheer;
Sweet gifts of grace shall come
And 'round her mind shall weave
Their ministering powers.
The glad earth shall receive
New brightness from her dowers,
And all the glorious thought
Transfigured, shall become
In words of beauty wrought
To bless her earthly home.
O take this gift divine,
A token from above,
As bright as stars that shine,
'Tis the *Ruby Flower* of love.

TO "BALSAM TREE" AND "SILVER STAR."

[Mr. and Mrs. Geo. A. Bacon, in commemoration of their Silver
Wedding. Oct. 14, 1882, by Ouina, through Mrs. Cora L. V. Richmond.]

I HEAR the chimes of Silver Bells wafted upon the
autumn air.
Weaving their soft, enchanting spells of memories
pure, sweet and rare.

They tell of marriage when life's morn was tinted with
a roseate hue,
When all embowered, to adorn the world. Love wove a
garland new.

They tell on one sweet Belle* whose love chimes as a
voice by heaven sent;
Whose undulations ever move in love and duty interblent.

The silver chimes go on and on, weaving sweet garlands
softly bright.
Like flowers the moonlight shines upon—like lilies near
an altar white.

They tell of later care and pain, of mist that must each
life enshroud;
But ever tell that love will give the silver lining to each
cloud.

They tell of labor well performed, of truths pursued— of
victories won,
Of hearts with sweet compassion warmed—of deeds of
kindness nobly done.

They tell of valiant words oft said for those in bondage
or in woe.

They tell of homage to the dead—(or those whom men
call dead below.)

Whose lives went out like shining stars to gleam more
silvery bright above.

But who on earth left silver bars of light to guide men
unto love.

They tell of aspirations pure—of conquest over selfishness;
Of friendship's flame that must endure, of hidden stores
of tenderness.

And this is wealth—altho' no hoard of miser's silver they
count o'er—
Their's is the hospitable board, love's latch-string ever at
the door.

Counting life's gain by what we give, their's is a Palace
Hall to-night;
Counting life's coin from "how we live," their coffers
shine with treasures bright.

Counting life's jewels by each thought, their's are as
"crowns of jewels" set
In life's pure silver—chastely wrought into this marriage
coronet.

And may the chimes go on and on until silver shall
change to gold;
Till all that memory shines upon shall not one shade of
tarnish hold.

Till everything hope holds before shall be enwreathed
with garlands bright;
And silver fountains that now pour, be merged in sprays
of golden light.

Chime on, O silver bells, to show how fair life's slow de-
scending way.—
Chime on, till all life's grain shall grow ripe for the GOLD-
EN WEDDING day.

*Daughter of Mr. and Mrs. Bacon.

MANZALIA.

[A Wild Flower of Colorado.]

———

ROUGH in the stalk and leaf,
    Up-reared from the dry sod,
Held sacred in a sheaf,
    The flower promised of God.

Waiting till noon is past
    And waning is the sun.
Then is its glory cast
    O'er the earth till day is done.

Starry, and snowy white,
    Manifold petals fair,
And stamens of pure light,
    Scent all the sparkling air.

Not one flower but a score,
    Large, starry-eyed and pure.
Followed by many more,
    They seem for aye to endure.

At early eventide,
    When stars blossom above,
Ye bloom here side by side,
    Symbols of Heaven's love.

And when the "stellar walk"
    'Lumines the heavenly way,
Ye shine forth from each stalk
    Like another "starry way."

How did ye learn to bloom
    Upon this barren land,

Lighting the desert gloom
  With glory of God's hand?

So do we learn to grow
  And light each desert place,
Until our lives shall glow
  Like you with Heaven's grace.

Manzalia, star of Heaven,
  Teach us thy lesson bright.
Until death's glorious even
  Guides us to flowers more white.

A CHRISTMAS STORY.

PART I.

NOW papa's not coming home and we can have no Christmas," said Freddie to Annie, as they sat by the fire in the sitting room, and Freddie began to have very gloomy thoughts indeed, he thought the world was not worth living in if there was no Christmas—mamma was sick and aunt Hilda said Santa Claus could'nt come that year because their papa was away; aunt Hilda ought to know for she was a great deal older than either Freddie or Annie, and must know more about Santa Claus; but why that good old fairy should stay away just because their papa was

gone, neither Freddie nor Annie could understand.

"Perhaps its because we don't have any fire
in the parlor now mamma is sick, and you know
papa had that chimney boarded up to keep out
the cold," said Annie; they both whispered, for
their mamma was sick, and was lying on the
bed in an adjoining room, but with the quick
hearing of love and illness she heard the eager
little voices and said:

"What are my darlings saying? Something
about papa I know, for I heard his name."
Annie and Freddie both stepped softly into
their mother's room, and said as they tenderly
kissed her, "Never mind mamma, we were
only saying how nice it would be if papa could
be here for Christmas," said Annie. "No mamma, / said," and Freddie felt half ashamed of
what he was going to tell, for he somehow
thought it would make his mamma feel badly,
"/ said I thought it was too bad we couldn't
have Christmas, because papa is away and
Santa Claus can't come." A look of pain did
cross the mother's face, but she smiled and
said:

"I know dears, it is hard for you, and lonely,
but let us try and out-wit Santa Claus this
time; suppose we try and think of something
nice to do for some one else, I don't mean to
buy something, but to *do* something and invite
Mr. Santa Claus just to drop in and take a rest

and get warm, but he needn't leave anything whatever. If we can only make up our minds to be happy *doing some good* for somebody; now will my little girl and boy try and have a 'merry Christmas' even if Santa Claus is *not* coming?' A bright thought had come to Annie, you could tell by the smile that came over her face, and when they kissed their mamma "good night," Annie called Freddie into the kitchen where they could talk and not be disturbed. Aunt Hilda had gone to attend to the invalid, and Betsey the house maid and cook, were asleep in the corner over the kitchen fire. Annie unfolded her plan to Freddie, at first he looked a little doubtful and puzzled, but soon his eyes sparkled and he entere l into her plans most heartily; it was a week before Christmas and they would have plenty of time. So when aunt Hilda came to put them to bed their tongues were busy telling her how they were going to "out-wit Santa Claus" and have a "merry Christmas" after all.

PART II.

THE next morning Annie brought out
the contents of a very small box, all
her earthly store, five dollars, hoarded
up from time to time; some portion
was a birthday present of one dollar,
other twenty-five cents and fifty cents
were little gifts of her papa at different times. Freddie brought *his* little penny
"bank" and found nearly two dollars. Aunt
Hilda was called into the council.

"Now," said Annie, "I want a nice warm·
wrapper for mamma and a pair of invalid slippers, how much will that take?" "Well," said
aunt Hilda softly, "I can get a very good one
for three dollars, and I will make it with Mary's
help. (Mary was a neighbor who always was
ready to lend a hand to anything good,) the
slippers I can manage alone."

"Then," said Annie, "we want to invite old
uncle Ben (the lame man you know,) and Mrs.
May the poor widow and her little girl Daisy,
and little Tommy the one-eyed boy, 'to tea,'
and we want a fire in the parlor so as not to
make too much noise for mamma." "And,"
said Freddie, "we want to *invite* Santa Claus
to tea but he needn't give us anything but you
know he gets very tired and cold." "And,"

chimed in Annie, "we want to make believe that papa is coming home and that we are doing it all for him, so please get his slippers and his dressing gown out of the closet and have them all ready, won't you auntie?"

"Is that all?" said aunt Hilda drawing a long breath, "you fairly take my breath away with your plans, but we will go and see what Betsey can do to help us." So they all went to the kitchen. Annie was quite sure she could help make the cake, and some nice biscuits for tea. Betsey assured her that she would do anything for a little queen like her, and Annie was so pleased. She and Freddie went to the grocery for all the things and aunt Hilda went to buy the material for mamma's wrapper. All was to be a secret from mamma, so Jim the colored man who did chores about the town, was brought to clean out the chimney and make the draft clear.

Everytime Annie and Freddie went into their mamma's room their faces were so happy she knew they had found something to amuse and please themselves with, half guessing that it was a secret from her she did not question them.

It was Christmas Eve, this was the night fixed upon for the party. The parlor fire was made, the company Annie and Freddie had invited were there.

"Uncle Ben" had a cheery face and altho' he

was alone and poor everybody loved him for he was so genial and good. "Havn't had such a Christmas Eve as this nigh on to forty years," he said as he drew near the fire and looked lovingly at Annie who ran and gave him a good hug.

Then came Mrs. May, pale and thin but smiling sweetly, with bright eyed little Daisy dancing by her side. Daisy had on a dress that had once been Annie's and it fitted that little lassie very well.

Mrs. May said to aunt Hilda, "How very kind it was of you to think of us, and your sister is sick too, I fear it will be too much for her to have all this confusion."

"O no," said Aunt Hilda, "This is the childrens' plan altogether, and it is to partly surprise their mamma that all this has been planned. She will be able to sit up and be brought in here in the rocking chair."

Then came little Tommy who had no home but was living with Mr. Brown the carpenter, he looked at the cheerful fire and recognizing Annie and Freddie came timidly forward when they asked him. The whole group looked happy. The tea table was spread in the parlor, and it made a pretty picture. When all was ready " mamma" (the invalid) was brought in wearing her new wrapper and slippers and looking very very happy. Freddie and Annie rushed to kiss her and tell her she looked "just lovely" in her warm wrapper (a wine color trimmed with soft velvet bands for collar and cuffs). Aunt Hilda placed a chair at the head of the table and put the dressing gown on the chair and slippers on the floor near for papa just as Annie had told her. The children were busy helping.

Just as they had all got seated and Betsey came in with the tea and biscuit "smoking hot," Aunt Hilda said:

"Annie and Freddie, you said you wanted Santa Claus to come and take tea. Are you quite sure you *do* want him? Would you not be afraid?"

"O please let him come, we only want him to get warm and have some tea," said Freddie.

"Well then," said Aunt Hilda, "will you, Freddie, go to the front door and say, 'Welcome, Mr. Santa Claus, come and take tea?'"

Without an instant's hesitation Freddie went to the door and said:

"Welcome, Santa Claus, come in to tea."

Some one *did* come in, but to Freddie's surprise instead of Mr. Santa Claus it was papa who clasped his little boy in his arms and then took Annie who ran to him saying:

"O papa, we only were 'making believe' give you a surprise party and you have really come." Aunt Hilda and mamma looked glad, but somehow not quite so surprised as the children. Then papa spoke to all the company

and sat down in his place, after first putting
on the dressing gown and slippers. *That* was
a happy Christmas Eve and uncle Ben told
stories and Mrs. May smiled while Daisy and
Tommy and Freddie had a game of their own
in the corner of the room.

Santa Claus *did* come that night, and Annie
told Freddie very confidentially when they
were looking over their Christmas presents the
next morning, that she believed Santa Claus
knew "all the time that papa was coming home."
Tommy and Mrs. May and Daisy and uncle
Ben all had a call from Santa Claus, mamma
looked "almost well" on Christmas day, and
papa said he wished they would *"just make believe"* surprise him every time he came home.

"Mamma," said Freddie on Christmas day,
"we have had a lovely time but we didn't out-
wit Santa Claus, no sir-ee."

Papa had changed his mind about coming
home, so while the children gave mamma a
"surprise" and made their friends happy by in-
viting them to tea. Mamma and aunt Hilda
kept it a secret from them that papa was coming.

But the children never knew how Santa Claus
found out that papa was coming home, and
that the parlor chimney was open for him to
come in.

PLAINS AND CANONS.

[A letter written by Ouina, through her medium, while in Colorado.]

—

EAR CHILDREN:—While "Water Lily" and "Sapphire" are out here in the clear air and pure sunshine of the plains and mountains; I think I will write about these wonderful "works of nature," and continue the story of *my* world when they return.

THE PLAINS

are wide continuous spaces free from verdure, except grass (sometimes) and a kind of whitish looking shrub called the "sage bush." The plains are not level, but undulating, yet when you look over them from a great distance they seem smooth. There are streams sometimes, and along these the trees flourish and the "ranch men" find water for their cattle. A "ranch" is a farm for sheep or cattle, and sometimes there are no buildings except a sort of hut built of the earth, with a roof, these are warmer in winter and cooler in summer than the "wigwams" of the pale faces. A few harvest moons ago the red men lived here and hunted the buffalo and the antelope for food, and built their tepes (wigwams) along the margin of the streams. The Utes, and Kiowas, the Cheyennes were here, each had their own hunting grounds; then they would come into the "foot-hills" and canons for rest and shelter from the storms, also for water.

THE FOOT HILLS

are little hills (they would seem quite large to you if placed on the prairie away from the mountains) that begin the mountains—just as you start and run a little, then go faster and faster until you go as swiftly as you can, so these small hills begin, and they go down and up, higher and higher, until at last the highest peaks rise above all others. Pikes Peak has many foot hills so you really cannot tell how high it is; but Cheyenne mountain, a little south of here, rises directly up from the plain like a huge wall, it has a very sharp ridge at the top and many queer shaped rocks that the storms have made.

THE CANONS

are gorges, or very deep ravines made in the sides of mountains by streams of water that forever flow down the mountain sides. These streams, caused by the melting snows, sometimes are mighty torrents and cut the rocks away; huge boulders are torn away from the great walls of rock by these streams, and always, even when but a little silver thread, the stream cuts and cuts. Some of these canons are several miles long and must have taken thousands of "harvest moons" to form. In the canons where there is moisture and shelter from the storms, all kinds of trees grow, large fir trees two hundred feet high, maple and birch, and many wild flowers, and along some of the canons little narrow "fire buffalo" trails three feet and a half wide, have been laid, so you can ride on the fire buffalo canoe and see the rocks tower a thousand feet above you. These are grand sights. Cheyenne canon is only a mile long, and one can easily walk there, following the stream first on one side then on the other, resting under the trees listening to the water as it leaps over the rocks or merrily flows along. I wish you were here and we would have a "nicpic" in Cheyenne canon; when the end of the canon is reached there is a round space something like a theater, and over one side the water comes down in three or four falls making a pretty picture. Now the stream is small because the snows are all melted on the mountains, but is never quite dry, and here on this large rock we will sit while we listen to the water and watch it as it tumbles down from the rocks above, and I will give you a poem.

IN THE CHEYENNE CANON.

MURMURING murmuring and murmuring forever,.
O silver threaded waters on thy way:
Why dost thou pause in thy falling never.
Why can no vast power bid thee stay?

As a silver line among the mountains,
As a flower of light falling from heaven,
O, thou mystic water of the fountains,
Tell us what the ages unto thee have given.

The water-fall answers, "I come from afar off.
My springs have risen on the far mountain's brow..
Seeking the ocean, toiling and toiling,
I never can rest, I must hasten e'en now.

"See where I have carved the vast precipices,
For ages and ages I struggle still on.
And plunging anon amid many abysses.
I have fallen in darkness, the sun shines still on

"Many places where often my waters have been,
And carved sweet places for the wild flowers to grow,.
The roots of the fir tree I murmurously lave.
And the wild birds here hasten, my song they well
        know.

"But oh! as the spirit must seek the eternal
By carving its way through the rocks of this earth,.
And at last findeth rest on the bosom supernal,
The ocean from whence all life must have birth..

"I have risen in mists and in vapor afar off;
I come as a spirit back again to the earth.
And now the eternal absorbs and claims me,
I hasten to where all the waters have birth."

BALD MOUNTAIN.

[Written by Ouina, through her medium while in Colorado.]

SILVER CLIFF, Colorado, }
20th, sun, 7th, moon, 1882. }

DEAR LITTLE CHILDREN:—This place is two thousand feet higher than Colorado Springs. "Water Lily" and "Sapphire" came here on the narrow Fire Buffalo trail the day before last Dod's day. They follow the valley to Pueblo and Canon City, then a branch of the trail winds up through the canon. I wish you could see the curves and windings, you would not think the fire buffalo could stay on the iron trail, but it does. The canon is narrow, and on each side the rocks and mountains *rise* very high, now like a smooth wall, and now jagged; the grade is up all the way, following the course of the stream for three hours, then they come upon this valley, which may properly be called a vale among the mountains, for although it is several thousand feet higher than you are, still there are mountain peaks 14,000 feet high (6,000 above this) visible from here. This place derives its name from a cliff which contains a large amount of silver, but it is "low grade" and they find it does not pay to work it. The valley itself is beautiful, and is about one thousand miles long and thirty miles wide, on every side are slopes leading up to the foot hills, and from some points here one can count six distinct ranges of mountains, one beyond the other. The town itself has little wigwams (dwellings) that look like boxes, some a little larger; but when the excitement of finding much gold or silver dies out, everybody goes away.

A little one side, but almost in the middle of this sloping valley, is a mound, or high hill, called Bald mountain; it is one mile from here to its base, and one mile from the base to the top, with a trail about two-thirds of the way. Yesterday Sapphire and Water Lily walked to the top and gazed on a beautiful picture. To the east was Pikes Peak,(for they are now on the other side of that range, having gone around it, first to the south, then west). To the north and west six or seven ranges were visible; to the west Horn's peak and many others, and far to the south a long range and the Spanish peaks. It seems that this must be a vast Temple in which to worship the Great Father. The clouds and storms keep close to the mountains and yesterday it rained and snowed on the mountains but was pleasant in the valley.

There are many wild flowers here; some that

are cultivated in the east, here grow wild, and
these make a bright carpet.

All over the plains and hill-sides one may
see little mounds of dirt and stones thrown up,
at first these might seem to be the holes of
some little animal, but they are "prospect
holes" dug by persons in search of veins of
gold or silver, and sometimes deep mines have
been sunk and abandoned, because, while there
are good "surface indications," there is not
much else. A little way from here (six or
seven miles) is the famous Basset mine, from
which several million wampums worth of ore
have been taken. Every body does not dig in
the ground; away over very near the base of
the mountains you will see trees and patches
of light and dark green, these are farms, or
ranches, where cattle, sheep, and poultry are
grown, and many vegetables, and where people live in funny log wigwams, but they have
pure air, and clear water from the snow-streams
flowing down the mountains; here the wild
birds love to come for shade and shelter, and
here sometimes are mountain deer and lion;
but these are not often seen since the pale face
came and drove the red man away.

BALD MOUNTAIN.

ALONE and lonely, all my sister hills
In vernal vesture cluster far away
Toward the mountians, they mid crystal rills
And fir-lined canons may together stay,
While I'm alone alway.

Around me sweeps the undulating plain,
Now green with summer, now with winter white :
The wild birds chant o'er me a sad refrain,
And pass along to valleys filled with light,
Nor heed my weary pain.

No verdure crowns me, a few flowers hide
In rocky shelter, and the wild birds' home
Is where the cooling streamlets ever glide,
Where bloom and leafy vestments gently come,
None linger by my side.

I see my brother mountains tower afar,
In solemn ranges sweeping to the skies ;
I watch o'er them the morn and evening stars,
And pillared clouds like gates of paradise,
From where my lone slopes are.

And yet for me the ancient earth has given
A crown of beauty that is all alone,
I too am of the earth, o'er me is heaven,
For me the purple mornings have their birth,
For me the snows are driven.

And I stand here to prove that loneliness
And lack of beauty are as near to God,
As peopled slopes where countless beings press,
As vernal ways by beauty's footsteps trod,
Nor ask I for redress.

The mornings and the evenings all are mine;
　The noondays and the starry, wondrous night.
The plains and flowers, and all things divine,
　That mark with change all things within my sight,
　　These, these are ever mine.

PICTURES ON THE WINDOW.

Painted by Jack Frost.

THEY woke one winter's morning,
　Hungry and cold, no food,
Nothing to make them warmer,
　No coals nor sticks of wood.

But they saw a bright face bending
　There above each window pane,
Now smiling and now touching
　Each glass with light again.

Who could it be so early,
　With pencils sharp and bright,
Making such strokes and sketches
　All in the dawning light?

Castles and towers and turrets,
　And mountains and ravines,
And horsemen riding swiftly
　Among the gorgeous scenes:

And vases full of flowers,
　And curtains of rich lace,
And fairies in sweet bowers,
　And many a lovely face.

Such pictures! stars and moons too.
  And frozen waterfalls,
And little children climbing through
  The farthest garden walls.

The sun arose and touched them,
  And lo! they fled away.
And a neighbor came to bring them
  To spend Thanksgiving day.

Busy with Jack Frost's pictures
  They forgot hunger and cold,
Till the sun's light and the love light
  Changed all their frost to gold.

—

THE STORM AT MANITOU.
(July 1, 1882.)

THE morn was fair, the sun-God rode
  In his bright chariot of gold
High to the zenith. O'er " Pike's Peak "
  A few light snowy clouds did hold
A fleecy veil; and " mount Cameron "
  Shone fair and bright in robes of green,
While the valley lighted by the morn.
  Nestled and smiled the hills between.

The healing waters seemed most bright:
  The village, *Manitou*, most fair;
And many sufferers came to drink
  And be made whole by the pure air.
Its crystal springs and wholesome food.
  Nature is kind to those who trust.

But she is fearful when the storm
  Sweeps o'er her bosom, yet God is just.

Mid-afternoon dark, lowering clouds,
  Lurid with lightning, hung above
The mountains, weaving fierce rain-shrouds,
  Until at last a sudden move,
A wild roar like the ocean wave
  Broke down the canon, and the wind
And waters came like beasts of prey,
  That no power whatsoe'er could bind.

O'er the stream's bed the torrent burst,
  Rushing and bearing rock and tree
Down through the dwellings, and the worst
  Was feared, who might in danger be;
When all around the tempest raged,
  And all beneath the waters rolled;
How soon the storm might be assuaged
  None knew, more dear than land or gold

Was human life! But a few moments, then
  The fierce demon had passed. Horses and kine
Stood buried neath the debris; carpets and floors
  Held tons of sand; ruin held riot fine.
No lives were sacrificed, as any knew;
  Friend drew nearer friend, thankful and blest
That when the air and earth to stillness grew
  All were together, and might calmly rest.

Two little boys had gone to walk and play
  Up William's canon in the morning light;
O'ertaken by the storm they cried for aid,
  But none were near, no succor on their sight
Dawned; when the cloud-burst came   [walls:
  They clung to an old lime-kiln's shelt'ring

But one, the weakest, smallest, could not hold,
　　The other powerless to heed his calls.

And when the storm was passed, the eldest clung
　　Still to the rocks for shelter, one was gone
And parents, friends followed the stream,
　　His little life amid the storm alone
Passed out, his body borne afar　　　[weep!
　　Was bruised and torn. O. mother, father,
And yet remember, where the angels are
　　They now your darling boy shall safely keep.

Next morn the sun-God shone as fair
　　As ever since the world of life began;
A Sabbath stillness filled the air;
　　Praises from tree and bird and man
Were wafted to the God above
　　For the bounty of his grace,
And pleadings at the Throne of Love
　　For his divinest grace.

But cold and still one little form
　　Rested anear the bleeding hearts.
No Sabbath sun could ever warm
　　Again his body, the piercing darts
Of anguish, rend the hearts that love,
　　But there is balm for every pain,
And in the spirit's home above
The loved are all restored again.

Restored ere then for earth and air.
　　Breathe of a presence all his own,
Anear them he may dwell more fair,
　　More loving now his spirit tone,
And when the clouds have rolled away
　　That hide the brighter light above,
Ye may behold him every day,
　　Made beautiful by death and love.

MANITOU'S GIFT.

T "Manitou" (the Father, the Mighty) are "healing springs," or mineral waters that bubble up from the earth, each spring has a different "medicine," soda, magnesia, salt, iron, sulphur and many other kinds of mineral, some of the waters are quite warm, and these serve for "baths." All these springs are near the foot of Pikes Peak, and several "hotel wigwams" have been built to accommodate the strangers and sick people who come for healing. There are drives and walks and trails up the mountains and canons, clear streams and beautiful flowers and trees are found here, and many huge rocks.

Manitou is the name of the village built near the springs, and the springs are named manitou, because the red man supposed the waters were a gift of the "Mighty Spirit" for the healing of the people," and I think they were correct in that belief.

ROSE OF LOVE AND DUTY.

[A Name Poem.—Given to Miss Phebe McCarroll, by Ouina,
through the lips of her medium, Water Lily (Mrs. Cora L. V.
Richmond), at Miss McCarroll's home, Ottumwa, Monday evening,
Aug. 28, 1882.]

IF truth and constancy could find
    Their fitting symbols on the earth.
And gentle duties that ever bind
    With thought of love, and worth:

If there was a name to typify
    The feet that ever willing go,
The hands ready to keep the heart
    That never moved slow.
The mind that steadfastly and still
    Pursues its silent will.

Then that would mean thy life :
    Thy heart is full of tenderness and care.
Of what may crown with beauty rife.
    The whole is beauteous unaware.

As the flower in its bloom
    Unconscious sheds its light.
So thy way gives to home
    Its mildness pure and bright.

Yet there is firmness, to dare, to do
    What seemeth right to thee.
To pierce all seeming barriers thro'.
    And set the spirit free.

Even love would not make thee go wrong.
    There might be sorrow's wound :

But the spirit will sing its truthful song.
Nor heed the worldly sound.

There is a hand extended near.
Like an artist painting with light.

Like a scroll of white thy spirit atmosphere.
Like flowers pure and bright.

And these, extended from above.
Typify thy faithfulness and love.
I give thee this for lines of beauty :
The *Rose of Love and Duty.*

SONG BIRD OF LIGHT.

A Name Poem;—Given to Miss Laura McCarroll by Ouina, through the lips of her medium, Water Lily (Mrs. Cora L. V. Richmond) at Miss McCarroll's home. Ottumwa, Monday evening Aug. 28th, 1882.

THE bird is made for singing;
　　Why shall it not sing?
The air is made for the winging,
　　For the flight of birds bright wing.
Why limit the air. and the song here?
　　The spirit its joys will shed:
Better the laughter than the tear.
　　And life brings a gentle tread.
As bright as the sunbeam glancing.
　　As the water free from care:
As fleet as the entrancing
　　April cloud so rare—

If sorrow comes, it touches
    But does not stay with thee.
It passes like a spring cloud,
    Leaving the spirit joyous and free.

Oh sing and dance in the sunshine,
    For this life is made of light;
But some where tender thoughts entwine,
    Beneath and out of sight.

For love is the prompting fountain,
    Though joy smiles in every glance;
Nor duties, nor sorrow's stern mountain
    Can stay, nor can woe here entrance.

Willing feet, and heart ever ready,
    Overflowing with deeds of pure love;
Hands full of kindness, and steady
    All thy labors in life here to prove.

Oh sing while the day is joyous,
    While the morning is full of light,
For life brings its lessons to each one,
    I name thee, the *Song Bird of Light.*

PEARL.

[A Name Poem, given to Miss Edna Douglas, by Ouina, through the lips of her medium Water Lily, Mrs. C. L. V. Richmond.

IF you will come with me where
   The song-birds are singing
    I will show you their place of rest.
    If you will come with me where their
  Wings are weary of winging
     I will show you a charmed nest.

Embowered within the solitude
   Sheltered within the lovely home.
Oh, come in the silence of the wood
   Where their sweet voices sing. Oh: come.

And there blooming on the ground,
   Full many flowers press:
And their streams, give a silvery sound,
   And from out the wilderness
Sweetest incense oft comes forth
   To beautify and bless the earth.

So is thy spirit gentle child
   As a song bird in its home.
As a wild flower blooming sweet and mild.
   Where daisy's footsteps come.

Affectionate and true and kind,
   Not forward, not over bold.
But seeking always the best to bind
   And sweetest flowers to hold.

And yielding within thy heart the grace
   Of each thy chosen place.

Oh I could name thee for many things!
   For the wild bird in the wood.

For the sweet waters murmuring
  That grace the solitude;

For the violets that shine and gleam
  Like the brightness of the sky,
For the roses that forever beam
  Proving that love is nigh.

But I will name thee what I see
  Within thy heart and life.
A Pearl; it is given for purity,
  It is a shield from earths strife.